Further Tales from a Male Nurse

Patrick K S Poon

First published in Great Britain in 2014 by
Patrick K S Poon

ISBN: 978-0-9575589-8-4

Printed by TJ International Ltd, Padstow, Cornwall PL28 8RW

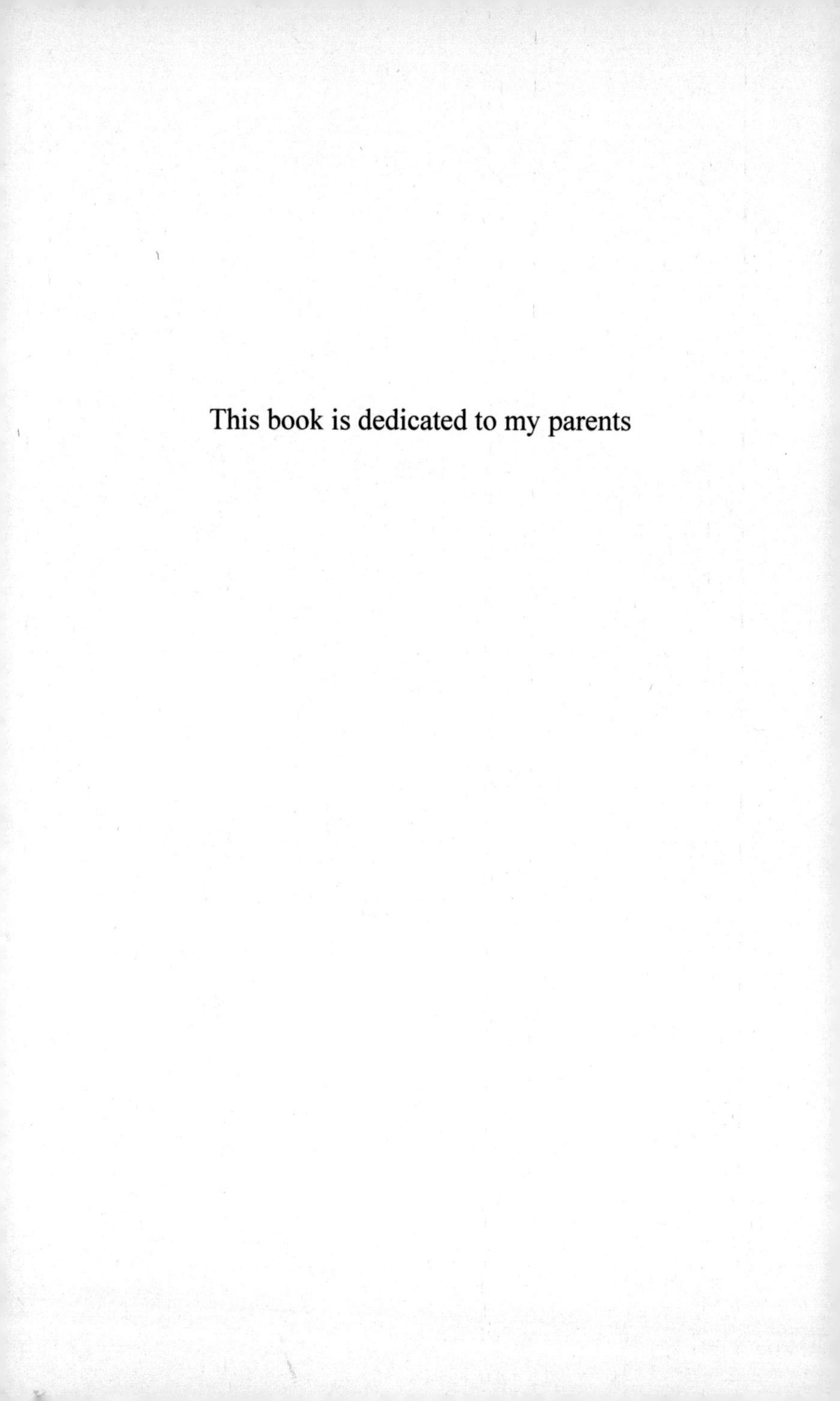

This book is dedicated to my parents

Acknowledgement

Special thanks to the help from Steve Sinfield and Diane Sinfield. Also sincere thanks again to Lindsey Faulkner for the artistic design of the book cover and the technical wizardry of help from Ryan, my eldest son.

Some of the tales are written with the help of research from various relatives and friends. Therefore, acknowledgement goes to the help and support to my brothers and sisters and spouses, George and Miranda, especially Sharon and her husband Peter Kwok. I would like to thank sincerely for the help to friends Graham Robinson, William McCauley, Paul and Rosemary Nicholls and Malcolm Russell.

Helpful support and encouragement and advice are appreciated and they are from Sue Brown, Jon Jacobs, Moya and Terry Middleton, Bob Quinney, Dottie, Peter and Lesley White, Rose and Paul Barklam. Not forgetting my family support from Jane, Ryan, Katherine, Thomas, Andy, Evan and Shauna.

Foreword

My first book,' Tales from a Male Nurse' that came out in April, 2013 has had a little success and has given me great satisfaction. Many friends have commented and suggested that I should write another one.

My mind went into overdrive but it went more smoothly than I expected. It really proves that every nurse has a tale to tell. Here is my second collection of true stories, mainly of tales of when I worked for the NHS and later in the nursing homes.

The journey of self publication has been an interesting and good learning curve in the world of books. One thing led to another and I was interviewed by BBC Radio Cornwall and Derby and my book is selling at Waterstones and Amazon.com and my website www.pkspoon.co.uk

I was even invited to the local NHS Fellowship for retirees at the local Plymouth branch. I was touched by the friendly support and the warmth given to me by the retired NHS staff, including nurses, administration staff, medical secretaries and estate staff whom I had never met before. But we spoke the same language, the NHS language. I was asked to talk about my book and I was also asked to read one tale from my book. I was pleased that it generated a good discussion and debate on the present state in the NHS in this country. God bless you all, retirees at NHS staff at Plymouth.

I am fortunate to have written the words in a favourable

writing environment in Cornwall. Inspiration comes smoothly when I look out of my windows to the tranquil moors, with its interminable horizon and the open azure sky. But I am still amazed that the memories come back as if it has been brooding and floating in my mind for many years.

All the names used are fictitious and any mistakes are mine.

Life is strange. One year ago, I would never have dreamt that I would be writing more tales in another book. I do hope that you enjoy reading them.

February, 2014.

Contents

Year 1970s

Tale 1

Reece's misfortune – 1982

'On the keyboard of life, always keep a finger on the escape key.'
Scott Adams.

I was a charge nurse on the surgical ward, on a late shift from 13.30-21.00 on a Saturday. It was a non-stop and relentless day with emergency admissions in a constant flow. Doctors and nurses were really working for the money.

Reece was admitted to be with an acute abdominal pain, a very common complaint that could mean anything. It could be due to severe constipation, acute appendicitis, cancer or stones in the colon. The possible causes were numerous.

He was about forty years old, rolling in acute pain and holding on his stomach. He was a thin man but he looked quite healthy. The doctor told me that he was vomiting lots of brown fluid, a sign of obstruction somewhere, not common in a young man. The doctor called that an acute abdomen, a tense and tender stomach pain. Has he perforated his stomach? It could be a possible cause. I was told that we had to 'prep' him for operative theatre as soon as possible.

One nurse had to shave him from nipple to knee as hairs could cause infection. He had to wait for four hours since he last ate so that his stomach was dry enough to be put on an intubations tube, a part of the anaesthetics routine. Then came my role to perform one of the most unpleasant procedures in nursing, so the patients told me. I had to pass a Ryles tube, a nasogastric tube via the nose to the stomach. I would not like to have it done to me.

In fact, many patients told me that they rather have a urinary catheter put in via the penis, a sharp but quicker procedure than passing the Ryles tube. A nasogastric tube was necessary to put into the stomach to empty its contents because the fluids inside would complicate any surgical procedure. The surgeon would like as little as possible in the stomach because it would help with the progress of the patients post-operatively. I set up my tray of equipment needed for the procedure.

I asked Reece to remove his glasses and just take a little sip of water to help with the swallowing, so that it would help with the the passing of the tube. I could not choose a thin tube as the man was not too little. I used a jelly lubricant to ease the tube into his stomach.

I advised Reece that it was an unpleasant procedure but the poor man had no choice. I asked Reece to try to swallow and took the sip of water and I inserted the tube up his nose. A bend was felt and I tried to curl the tube round it and I could see his eyes watering. I persisted but he was coughing a lot, indicating the tube might have gone to his windpipe so I withdrew the tube and tried again. The second attempt succeeded and I passed the nasogastric tube successfully through his nose into his stomach. I withdrew his stomach content into a kidney dish where I placed a piece of litmus paper: the paper turned from blue to pink, meaning its acid content would indicate the tube was in his stomach.

'Sorry, Reece for doing this to you.' I apologised as a matter of routine. Many patients told me on discharge that was the worst procedure done on the ward, worse than coming round after surgery.

'Okay. You have to do what you got to do.' He was wiping tears from his eyes. I hoped that the cause of his obstruction would be curable. One cause could be the twisting of the bowels inside as he'd had his appendix removed some months ago. However, he felt better with the stomach content emptied out. In fact, the tube was put onto continuous drainage into a sealed bag. A fair amount of brown colour content was drained out to the bag, no wonder he was feeling a little better. He was showing signs of dehydration because he was feeling weak with dry skin and he was in shock meaning that his blood pressure was low and pulse fast. An intravenous drip was put up to give him fluids and so compensate for the loss. His wife was told to that he would need an emergency operation to see what was happening inside. The Xray showed some signs of intestinal obstruction, a very common emergency admission.

During the operation, it was found that Reece had some adhesions; some bowels had got stuck together, causing the obstruction. And the adhesions were caused unintentionally by the previous operation, the removal of the appendix. This condition was not very common but it had happened to poor Reece. But he was fortunate that it was not cancer and he was relieved. The situation had happened fairly suddenly and he felt so ill that he thought he was going to die.

His post operative progress was so good that soon he was allowed to have his intravenous infusion and nasogastric tube removed. Reece was feeling so relieved as I took his tubes out. He started his intake of fluids, then a soft diet and normal diet and soon he was on the way to recovery.

'Worst thing that happened to me, this nasogastric tube through my nose.' he said. I agreed wryly.

I knew of two situations that trainee nurse's quitted nursing because of certain nursing work was not for them. One was this passing of the Ryles tube. We were not tough nuts really but somehow we could do it for the good of the patients.

Tale 2

Henry's lesson – 1978

'Each man is the architect of his own destiny.'

It was a fairly warm morning in May. I was off duty and I was strolling down to the busy town of Walsall, wanting to treat myself with a new shirt. A thin tall young man was approaching me and greeted me.

'Good morning, Patrick. How are you?'

His face was fresh and happy and I remembered the face, perhaps not so well that I could not remember his name.

'You cannot remember me, can you, Patrick?'

'I am sorry but your face looks familiar.'

'It is Henry, your regular overdose patient on your ward.'

'Well, you look so well. I am pleased you stop to say hello. What are you doing now?' I was so pleased to see him looking so well that I shook his hands. The words of 'regular overdose' reminded me only of one name.

'I'm studying computer science.'

'That is good news.' I recalled that once upon a time, he was very defiant and against everything and everybody. The whole world was against him at that time.

'And thanks to your help too, Patrick.'

'Well, what did I do?' I could not remember what I did.

'Well, you probably did not know. This happened some five months ago on your ward; you introduced me to a dying young man who died of leukaemia later.

Henry told me the story as in the following. I was glad that he told me because I did not know his side of the full story …

*

I was on duty one Saturday afternoon and I was told that we had a regular overdose a young man to be admitted. He took some sixty paracetamols and was unconscious. He had a stomach washout and his levels for the paracetamols were not too bad. So I was informed that we just watched him and had been on intravenous fluids to compensate the fluid loss. When we were told his name, we were all very quiet.

On the ward, we knew Henry well. He was admitted three times before with similar overdose and we recalled quite distinctively that he enjoyed the stomach washout which we found unusual. How could one enjoy a thick tube passed to your stomach and wash it all out with fluids and be sick afterwards? Strange young man, we thought.

For many routine overdose patients admitted during the weekend, they would have to wait for a psychiatrist to see him on a Monday late afternoon. During the admissions, Henry never waited for a psychiatric review on a Monday evening. He just discharged himself by signing a shelf discharge form. Henry came from a well-to-do family. After his admissions, there were always many well dressed adults around, wanting to see him. But one could tell that he did not get on well with them. He blamed everyone for what he had become. One could also tell he was stubborn. But he only knew that he was poor but he had no support from home. He simply did not want to listen to anyone.

This kind of admission sometimes showed that the patient wanted attention from a wrong way but he did not want to die. He told us that he did not know what he wanted and wished he was dead though we knew that he did not really want to die. So, when he knew he was coming in again, we were fed up with him really and we would have to go through the circle game of the procedure again.

'To check his level of paracetamols okay, wait till he was conscious, feed him well and once he is okay, discharge him after the psychiatrist visit.' That was the doctor's instruction that we knew by heart. And we knew that he would not wait and would probably discharge himself before Monday evening. We were cynical that he was just wasting our time and money from the NHS.

By Saturday evening, he woke up half asleep. He was looking around and could see we were very busy, rushing about to have different jobs done.

'Are you okay, Henry?'

I asked but I did not have much time to spend with him because many other patients seemed to require more urgent attention and more ill than him.

'Yes, you seem busy, Patrick.'

I nodded. In the previous three admissions over nine months, Henry's admission seemed to happen at a less busy time and we had time to chat about his problems and we reassured him but all was to no avail. On this very afternoon, we had four admissions; all nurses were running off our feet, tending to other patients' needs. Henry was on the first bed in the front bay so we could observe him easier.

A scream of agony pierced from the side room near him and it drew Henry's attention. I went in to see if Mark, another young patient, was okay.

'I am in severe pain. Could I have some stronger painkiller injection?' He pleaded.

'Of course, it has been more than four hours. Is the pain bad?' I asked, showing my sympathy.

'Dreadful.' Mark was also having a blood transfusion and he looked pale and very thin. His voice was weak. The curtain was not drawn properly and Henry could see him.

I checked the controlled drug of morphine for Mark with another nurse and we both went in to witness the injection given. That was the rule for the controlled drug to be given. Controlled drugs were drugs made of heroin which was used effectively as a painkiller and it also made the patient euphoric. It worked on Mark and he was thankful for our help.

I came out of the side room, feeling sad for Mark. He was so young and had done no wrong to anybody. Why was he so ill at so young an age? I was a fool to think like that, especially for a male ward sister like me. I should have been harsher.

Henry somehow saw me, feeling so sorry for him. Perhaps it was an expression that Henry never saw in me.

'Are you okay, Patrick?' Henry asked.

'Yeah.' I said, unconvincingly.

'What is the matter with him? He is so young.'

'I am not allowed to tell you but he is very ill.'

'Tell me, Patrick, I am old enough to face the dawn.'

I thought a little and told me, 'He has got leukaemia and he is very poorly.' Perhaps I should not have told him that either.

'So I can see. How old is he?'

'Same age as you. Twenty-two.'

'Really, he looks like 30 years old.'

'Henry, if you think you are hard done by in life, look at him. He looks ghastly.' I should not have said that.

'Can I talk to him?'

'Not sure, I better ask him.' I replied,' Perhaps it might give you company this weekend.'

Later on, I did ask Mark if he would talk to Henry and he agreed. I knew on that Sunday, they had had many discussions in Mark's side room. I was glad they talked and perhaps it helped them somehow. They seemed to get along and had a long conversation.

I worked on a Monday till 16.00 and I was pleasantly surprised that Henry agreed to stay on to see the psychiatrist that evening. I had Tuesday and Wednesday off and when I came back on duty. Henry was discharged and Mark survived for another five days and passed away peacefully.

Henry told me that he did go back to visit Mark as his visitor on a Wednesday before Mark died. During their conversation, he told me that he was really told off by Mark to get a life and he must not waste his life. Mark wished he could live like Henry and if he did, he would have made a life for him.

This unplanned event gave Henry a lesson in his young life. It made him look at things very differently. On reflection, I was glad about what I did. Unintentionally, I gave Henry an opportunity to learn a lesson about life. It worked very well for Henry but I was sorry that Mark had never been given a chance in life though.

Tale 3

Love and lust on the wards

'First cut is the deepest' ...

In my first book 'Tales from a Male Nurse', there were two tales from my good old Chinese friend Chan who was a charge nurse. We were close friends and often met up to gossip about our work and life in general. We often had a pint of shandy and enjoyed each other's company. He once told me of tales of love and lust on the wards, like one would do with a male friend.

When he was starting his new training at Kettering he found the town full of young trendy people. People commented that with all these good looking young women at the hospital, they attracted young men in droves. When one turned up to work at 7.30 in the mornings, young men were often seen leaving the nurses' home. Love or lust was in the air.

On the course of the student nurse training, Chan was required to go to St. Crispin's Hospital at Northampton for three months of psychiatric nurse training. Northampton was some ten miles away. The mental hospital was very large in those days, in comparison with the general hospital. His work was on a schizophrenic ward. Compare with a general hospital, there was much less physical work to do as most patients could look after themselves. The patients suffered from psychoses, neuroses and there were drug addicts too. He was allocated to work with a black nurse called Lindsay who was young, friendly and had a lovely figure. Her breasts showed tightly under her uniform. She was nice to him and he seemed to be working the same shifts as her most of the time. It seemed that they were close to each other in their off duty times too.

After a few days of work with her, they seemed to understand each other very well. They liked each other's company. She was telling him that she lived nearby and she had only one more year to finish her training. She could not wait to be a staff nurse.

One afternoon he was with her helping her to bathe a male patient. The patient was very quiet, disillusioned with the world and he seldom spoke. If he did, he was talking to an invisible person. He was in the bath, enjoying the water and Lindsay was gazing through the window.

'What are you looking at?' Chan asked curiously.

'Have a look!' Lindsay replied.

They could see a charge nurse of the adjacent ward in his office. He had locked the door an attractive female nurse was sitting opposite him. They were talking, enjoying each other's company. She giggled and drew closer to the charge nurse. He undid the zip at the front of her uniform. She did not resist and her hand was moving towards the zip of his trousers.

Underneath her uniform, she had a full figure. She allowed him to undo the front hook of her bra. She was smiling as he kissed and sucked her breasts.

'My goodness, how long has this been going on, Lindsay?'

'About two weeks and usually at this time!!'

'Oh, he is a nice guy.'

'Yes, a married man of two kids.'

'Mm, I have not seen the nurse before.'

'She is from another ward, a good looking single girl.'

'Right?'

'And she is good in bed.'

'Right.' Chan did not know what to say to that.

The nurses in the office did not have sex though they continued caressing each other and kissing seductively.

Chan had not seen such lascivious life activity before and he became quiet.

Lindsay turned to him and said, 'Do you think that I have a good figure?

'Yes, you are beautiful.' Chan was a little panicky as he had never been asked this sort of thing before. As she drew her near, he touched her breasts. They were tender but firm and she seemed to be enjoying the feel. Chan went further and was quite excited.

'They are lovely; you are beautiful.' He said.

Lindsay did not resist but drew closer. Chan undid her front buttons and saw her black bra; he took her breasts out of her bra and kissed her nipples. She was relishing the feel and murmured in ecstasy. The patient was quiet, still enjoying his bath, living in his own world and was totally unaware of things happening near him.

After ten minutes of frolicking with Lindsay and watching the nurses across the way to finish their sexual act, Chan was a little out of breath. He was not used to these activities in the hospital.

'Come to me tonight on C block.' Lindsay suggested.

'Ok.'

'I bet you are good in bed.'

'Mm…' was all that he could say.

The shift ended quickly. That night, Chan dressed himself trendily and went to C block where the female nurses lived. He was wondering what would happen. Lindsay might be that kind of girl, just wanting a good time with him or perhaps she knew he was an innocent. He saw her in the lounge in the nursing home. She was with a group of girls who lived there. They were drinking and there was loud music in the air.

'Hello, Chan, good to see you. What are you doing here?' She seemed to be a bit drunk.

'Just wandering…' He was speechless.

Chan soon said hello and left the nurses home. He thought that perhaps he was taking things too seriously and that he was inexperienced in this kind of thing. In a way, he was relieved that nothing had happened.

*

At Kettering, the student nurse training was good. Chan enjoyed his experience of working and living there and for four months, he had to be on night duty on a surgical ward.

Chan tended to be on duty more with two part time staff nurses, staff nurse Bayliss and Denise. The former was a comely, middle aged lady, a good and experienced nurse who taught him a lot on surgical nursing. Chan enjoyed her company and she was kind and helpful to him.

Staff Nurse Denise was better looking and in her late twenties. The white uniform she wore showed her good figure and her style of her lovely brown hair matched perfectly to the shape of her face. She was a fast and efficient worker like Chan. For two weeks, Chan worked with her all the time and they got on very well.

With her, Chan had the habit of singing the song, 'we will' by Gilbert O'Sullivan.

Dense used to say, 'Will we?'

Chan smiled.

'You like that song, don't you?'

He nodded.

'You are an unusual guy, aren't you?'

'In what way?'

'I heard that you do not go out with many girls here.'

Chan shrugged. Perhaps he had not found a right girl.

'And you read poetry!'

'How do you know that?'

'Staff nurse Bayliss told me. I have never known a male nurse to be interested in that sort of thing.'

'Sorry.'

'Don't apologise, you are lovely guy and you are good to the patients too.'

'Thanks.'

'And you were reading words from Rod Mckuen.'

'You know his songs and lyrics?'

'Not very well.'

I hummed his songs with the right rhythm and it was catchy.

'Lovely song and words…..I heard it before.'

'Tom Jones sang a good version of the song.'

'Right.'

'Next time you are on with me, I shall take you some poems to read…'

'Oh…………'

The following week, Chan took her poems by Keats, and some lyrics of Bob Dylan and Leonard Cohen. Denise seemed to be friendlier with him and after work was done for the night he would put his arms around her and his legs on her lap. They were getting familiar with each other and they seemed to enjoy each others' company.

'Do you always do things like this to staff nurses?' she asked.

'No, only to you because you are special.'

She smiled and enjoyed the frolics but she had two children and seemed happily married, so she told Chan. They both did not know what to do.

Chan tried to kiss her but she deliberately avoided him. There was a good sparkle between them but she was some ten years older than him and she was married. It reminded him of the movie 'tea and sympathy' that a young boy was in love with a teacher's wife.

Chan's last week of night duty came though he wished it was not as it meant he would not see Denise again. They would have only two more nights together. She came on duty on the last night with make-up on and she looked really beautiful. It was the first time she had the make-up on for Chan. Chan was besotted and he had never had such a strong feeling for a woman before.

The night went on too quickly. Soon they did their work and all the patients were asleep.

'You look sad, Chan.' She said.

'You know the reason. Can I see you during the day please? Have a lunch with me.'

'Not a good idea. I am a married woman. You will find a nice girl soon.'

Chan held her in my arms and kissed her lips. She returned his kiss tenderly and looked away, 'You have to forget me, you know. And we must not do anything else.'

He did not say anything. She kissed him tenderly on the face, 'You are a nice man. If I was not married, I would go with you.'

For the first time, Chan put my hand on her breast. Her uniform was thin and he could feel the firmness. She did not take his hand away but put her head on his chest. A patient rang the bell and interrupted the moment. Denise went to see to the patient.

The night dragged on and they embraced and hugged together many times as if they did not want the night to end. But it did end and Chan had never felt so sad in his life. His world collapsed when he left her that morning. They said a simple farewell and he did not see her again.

'First cut is the deepest' are the words that Chan could always remember when this episode of the life happened. He thought that he was truly in love but it was with a married woman and it was not to be.

Tale 4

The happiest nursing days in casualty, Kettering General Hospital 1973 – 1974

'Perfect happiness, even in memory, is not common.'

Jane Austen

I was a third year student and was allocated to casualty at Kettering General Hospital, waiting for my final result. Colleagues said the casualty was a nice place to work in and the staff was nice. Sister Parry from Wales, the senior sister in charge, was a small lady and a spinster. It was said that she had been awarded an OBE for her services to nursing.

There was Mac, a charge nurse who had the reputation of being friendly. He enjoyed teaching students. He was half Chinese and half Irish and we got on very well because he was raised for many years in Hong Kong. We talked about our good times in the colony and Mac always enjoyed his char siu bao (roast pork bun) for his breakfast and I liked it too. I looked up to him as my mentor in nursing because he was very good with patients, especially the children. He had good social skills and I have copied his style in nursing and social care in my nursing career.

In those days, we were allowed to plaster fractured limbs and to stitch simple wounds on hands and the head. During my stay there, he taught me about many different surgical procedures and I followed him around so that he would allow me to practise these tasks.

Another very friendly member of the staff was Jenny from Australia. She was working there as a touring nurse to visit parts of England. Her husband was a doctor and they both used their profession to work and tour UK. She was always by my side by giving me those plastering, stitching jobs to do and I really appreciated her help. With all these friendly and good staff, no wonder casualty was one of the most popular allocations in the eyes of the students.

I was very keen on learning new things and perhaps there was why Sister Parry started to be very nice and friendly towards me. Gossip started that I was her 'blue eye' boy. I have had many very good students' reports with each allocation but I had never received the 'blue eyed boy' status before. Gradually, I became part of the team in casualty. They were very thrilled for me when they heard that I had passed the examination and had become a state registered nurse.

I had difficulty arranging with the hospital switch board to ring home to Hong Kong to relay the good news. Sister Parry used her influence to arrange it for me. In those days, when I told to my parents about my good news it cost me one pound per minute. But it was worth it because my family was very happy for me. It is a wonder that nowadays one can ring on the mobile phone to any part of the world for much more cheaper price.

There was a vacancy in the casualty and they asked me to apply for it and I got the post easily because I got on so well with the staff there. I had to say that I worked hard and liked the jobs that I did. It was wonderful to feel that I was qualified and now a staff nurse in the department that I loved. I enjoyed teaching the student nurses too.

During the year in casualty, I learnt how to set up trolleys and trays for minor operations such as close reduction of a fracture and manipulation of fractures and many different procedures. An opportunity arose that I could apply to do a diploma in a nursing course which was deeper and a valuable course in nursing for trained nurses. I applied and got on it to do the course for free it was intense but very interesting.

The staff was good at teaching student nurses and I have been influenced by them. The role of staff nurse was fulfilling though it was not as responsible as a charge nurse. Whatever the problem with patients and students was, I could refer it to the nurse in charge, namely a ward sister or charge nurse. I was a staff nurse for two years before I had a promotion as a charge nurse. As a charge nurse, I was in charge all the time, the buck stopped with me and it was up to me to deal with the problem. As a staff nurse, I was so carefree. It was the happiest period of my nursing career.

Casualty might not be every nurse's favourite but it was mine. I liked the emergencies of the unexpected, the excitement, and the urgency of helping some one in need. The doctors and nurses worked very well as a team and patients were very grateful for the help they received.

I was happy in casualty for one year and then I started work on the orthopaedic ward. I was there learning as a staff nurse because I knew that there was a post of sister become available. I did apply but did not get the post. I was disappointed but the nursing officer of the orthopaedic unit suggested that

I went back to casualty department. I agreed even though my ego was bruised.

It was very good of the Sister Parry and Charge nurse Mac to have me back as a staff nurse for they knew that I would apply elsewhere for a promotion. They were protective towards me and somehow they treated me like a member of the family.

I did apply and got an interview and I was successful in becoming a charge nurse on an acute medical ward in Walsall, West Midlands.

When I left casualty, I kept in touch with Mac and I am still in touch to this day. He is in his eighties now and I have visited him every now and then and we always exchange Xmas cards. We still talk about old Hong Kong where he lived for some years and I told him about the changes there after my frequent visits there. Mac also visited Hong Kong a few years ago and he showed me photos of his visit. It was good to keep alive our friendship.

I learnt that Sister Parry passed away some years ago in Wales, and Mac however was quite well, despite his old age. Whenever I watch television programmes like ER (Emergency Room), I always recall the good times I had with Mac and Sister Parry.

4A

Underground poem

Terminal 5, Heathrow airport.

Last October sitting at the Heathrow airport,
I saw a metal bin.

I was writing a poem then,
feeling moody and literate within.

The words flowed on and on,
like the lyrics in a song.

Then I saw the side of the same bin,
labelled 'underground poems wanted, please put within.'

So I finished the poem
and popped it in.

Saint Dominick, Cornwall.

Patrick K S Poon.
23.2.2014.

Year 1980s

Tale 5

Sickness record in the NHS

'If you want a job done, ask a busy person.'

It was often said that sickness records in the NHS were poor because staff members were stressed. Whilst most of the sickness absences were genuine, some were quite doubtful. It might have been the responsibility of my being in charge of the ward that I felt that I must turn up to work to fill in. If I did not, we would be short staffed; nurses would struggle to fulfil the work and patients suffered.

Once, I had a very unusually appreciative Divisional Officer in Nursing who wrote me a letter to thank me for not being off-sick for three years. He said that though he was not allowed to give me any financial reward, he was thankful for my work ethic.

Sister Smith was in charge of the gynaecological ward and everyone knew she was often off sick, using dubious excuses. Unlike a private company, she would still get paid. With her pattern of sickness, the second ward sister was grumbling because she had to work harder if I could not find her any help from other wards. Twice, I had to see Sister Smith regarding her sickness record when it showed that she only worked one full month in an eight month period, and then she improved a little.

Charge Nurse Sam was from India and in charge of a surgical ward. Clinically, he was efficient and experienced. He could talk till the cows came home and a bit of a 'know-all'. Smartly dressed, he was quite tall and really fancied himself, so the female nurses told me. He was separated from his wife and had a young son and so his home life was complicated.

He was off sick quite often, using small excuses like a blocked nose. At times, when he could not find anyone to baby-sit his son, he rang to say that he was stressed and did not turn up to work. It was very difficult to find someone to be in charge of a surgical ward so often.

In 1985, the nursing officer was in charge of some wards. When he or she was not on duty, and he would leave his 'bleep' to a ward sister and he would deal with any problems. This was a common practice and worked well. Ward sisters had no problems in tackling the problems because normally, there were no problems. Any foreseen problems would be resolved by the nursing officer before he went home. Normally, the nursing officer ensured that there was a ward sister to take the 'bleep' to cover the unit. I was a surgical Nursing Officer then.

Sam's sickness record was very poor and I had to see him with his problem as it was mentioned in the disciplinary procedure. He explained that he was sorry that he only worked one full month in eight, because he did not plan it and his absences were genuine. But it was all uncertificated sickness and it was always one or two days off sick. He said that he would rather work than being off sick. I said that this was happening in the last eighteen months and I had to report it to the Director of Nursing Officer (DNS) as stated in the procedure. He shrugged his shoulders and left the office.

The DNS saw Sam about his poor sickness record and

I met him in the corridor. He told me that he was not happy because it smacked of racial discrimination. I wondered if it was because of the DNS was English. The DNS told me that Sam would be written to about the interview and he would be soon given a first warning if he did not improve in three months.

Two days later, Sam was off sick with a medical certificate, stating stress was the reason. One week later, the DNS asked to see me in his office.

'How are things, Jack?' I asked the DNS, a fair built man of few words. The staff was not sure they liked him. He was pleasant but distant. Perhaps he had to be with his senior position. But he was a shrewd man.

'Not good. I just had a call regarding Sam's sickness.'

'OK, where from?'

'The Racial Discrimination Board.'

'Really?' I was surprised because I could not see any act of discrimination at all.

'What did they say?'

'They reckon that we were against him because of his dark skin. He thought that he was also unfairly treated and they said there was an issue about the evening bleep rota, he was hardly put on the bleep to be an acting nursing officer.'

'That is ridiculous. He was taking my bleep many times.'

'He reckoned that because of his colour, he was taking the bleep less because the other ward sisters were English.'

I was speechless. In fact, many ward sisters or charge nurses preferred not to have the bleep as it could give them more hassle and there was no financial reward for taking the bleep but it does give one management experiences.'

'And the demand is ridiculous from this Board.' The DNS

went on, 'They want me to give them an explanation why we left others with the bleep and not him in your unit for the last two years. And this applies to the medical unit, elderly care unit and theatres and the children's unit because there might be a trend to discriminate against black staff members.'

I did not know what to answer; the task would be enormous.

'And,' The DNS went on, 'This might mean lots of work for many officers of the units.'

'So, what shall we do?'

'I would suggest doing nothing. I do not want other nursing officers to do all the unnecessary work. And I think Sam will leave.'

'Oh.' I could understand the dilemma and I said, 'With Sam's work history, he will not stay long. He has worked at many hospitals in the last ten years.'

'I know. I have checked. Let's us leave it at that and do not say anything to Sam about this. And I will not reply back to the Board either. Let see what will happen.' He suggested.

Jack, the Director of Nursing Services, was correct. We did not do anything proactively. Sam's sickness record improved a little but then he left. He'd stay only two years in the hospital.

In the NHS, some staff members would know how to use their position, be it their colour or gender to get things their own way. The NHS was a big organisation and to manage it required many different strategies.

Tale 6

Regional illnesses

'There but for fortune, go you or I …'

I am sure many nurses and doctors know that some diseases are related to specific locations.

My first hospital in England was in the sleepy town of Newmarket where is renowned for horse racing. Hence, it was not surprising to know some patients were admitted because of falls from the horses. Once we had a very bad road traffic accident when people were travelling to race meetings. Weekends drunks were commonly admitted in those days as are to-day. Many people got paid on Fridays and much money was splashed out on drinking. I was surprised at this habit because I grew up in the Far East; it was not a common practice. Drinking alcohol seemed to be a culture here. The Newmarket General hospital is no more: the building is now a nursing home.

At Kettering Hospital, , my next place of work, illnesses or disease admissions were not so specific to the area except it was near the steel town of Corby where many Scots lived. The Scottish workers liked a drink and drunken behaviour was very common. In those days, it was not unusual for us to find beds in the corridors, full of drunks from Corby. In those days in the 1970s, it was official practice that once a patient had lost a moment of consciousness; he would have to remain in hospital overnight so that he could be observed in case he had any cerebral haemorrhage. 5% of the patients admitted did bleed in the brain following falls. In these cases, they would require an emergency operation. Surgeons would drill holes in the skull to get rid of blood clots.

Steel industry related accidents happened quite often too. I recall once when I was working in casualty, there was a poor man who had an arm sawn off at work. Many staff was reluctant to see the arm in a box, except a young houseman and myself.

In those days, I had friends who worked in Colchester. They told me that they lived near universities where many idealistic young people lived. Weekend admissions were common for cases of drug and alcohol abuse. It was commonly known that these youngsters wanted to protest about the systems not working fairly in the country and they wanted to seek attention.

When I had my first promotion to be a charge nurse at Walsall, I came across many illnesses caused by poverty. Walsall was then and even now, a very deprived area. The Manor hospital where I once worked had been a workhouse. However, I owed much of my professional knowledge in nursing to this hospital. Here, I came across tuberculosis, scabies, epilepsy, asthma, heart attacks, lung diseases, severe hepatitis due to swimming in dirty water nearby, aortic aneurysms, cancers of all types and surgical complaints. Indeed, many of my tales were from this hospital. I had a very fruitful eleven years working there and learning my profession. I met many good and saintly doctors and some strange ones too.

When I moved on to Burton upon Trent as an assistant

director of nursing services, I was in charge of the Burton General hospital. This place does not exist any more; it has been demolished. I learnt many of the signs and symptoms of different diseases too. I used to frighten some student nurses as I liked to do ward rounds with them and liked to know the diagnosis of the patients. So when some students saw me approaching, they would quickly go and hide or they tried to read up what was wrong with the patients beforehand. This was said to me by a senior tutor from the local college of nursing, some time later.

I learnt however then, in 1988, it was not surprising to see young men unconscious and dying of oesophageal varices. These men were lying there, because they had drunk too much in their younger years. Burton-Upon-Trent was a brewing town, successful because of the pure water, making Bass lager. In those days, brewery workers could have free beer to take home. They had many drinking-related diseases and some of them drank themselves to death.

According to the British Medical Journal, the five common causes of death in England were heart diseases, cancers, road traffic accidents and the suicide of the youngsters. The last of these I found to be particularly sad. The suicide of the youngsters, especially young men, has been on the increase for many years. The stress of working life and the stress of unemployment were both to blame. It was certainly a complicated matter to resolve.

Tale 7

A macho Chinese on the ward

'The reverse side also has a reverse side'
-a Japanese proverb.

I have always been interested in writing. When I was a teenager in Hong Kong in the 1960s, I was a big movie fan. I was also a student, enjoying reading a students' newspaper called 'Students' weekly.' There was always a column about movies. One December, I wrote an article on the best ten films shown of the year. It was published and I got paid $6 for it. I was so happy to see my name in print. I showed that to my father and he smiled. He read it and nodded his head.

My writing bug stayed with me for many years. I wrote some short stories and had many rejections. One day, on the way back on the plane in Hong Kong in 1990, I was reading a Chinese Newspaper, 'Ming Pao' which was a very popular newspaper. It was asking writers to share their experiences abroad. So I tried and sent them three articles.

Four months later, I received a bank draft from the newspaper for two articles; I was so thrilled and rang my brother, asking him to search my articles. He sent them to me and I was again excited to read my name in print. I did not know what the circulation of this newspaper was and who might be reading it. Two years later when I visited my hometown of Hong Kong, an old friend who I always met had saved the cutting of the article and showed it to me. I was amazed.

I was telling this writing experience to a Chinese friend at Walsall and he told me about the Chinese Times, the Siyu, based at Manchester which was publishing articles in English and Chinese in the newspaper and was asking for contributors. I rang the editor and he asked me to write two articles. I did and I got accepted. From then on I wrote for them regularly for four years.

The writing experience opened another horizon for my restless mind. I entered some competition in Chinese and won the third prize. I was really surprised as my writing in Chinese was not that good. However, I did have many articles published in English also. For those four years, I was feeling proud to see my articles printed in English and Chinese and I had a bi-monthly column. My topics were usually on health matters, the movies and some Chinese children's stories. To these days, I still possess a scrapbook of my work.

One of the articles was on nursing, a factual story, was it was published in March, 1994 in Chinese. I have translated into English.

*

'A macho Chinese on the ward in the hospital.'-1990.

My friend, Mr. Chan, was a nice friendly man. He was always helpful and kind to us. We used to play machong together and we had great fun. We listened to Hong Kong songs and we conversed in Cantonese. It was good for us to speak in our native tongue and we enjoyed some home cooked Chinese food.

Chan was definitely the head of his household and would not be overruled by anyone; his wife was meek and subservient. He was always in a good health but one day, he had a fall and hurt his back. He was sent to hospital and to have complete bed rest which was not easy for Chan as he had always an energetic man. Moreover, he was ruled by nurses who were females. That was not a done thing in his book. In his world in China, men should always rule the roost.

He spoke a little English, like many Chinese of his generation. When he got frustrated, he would ring me up and I would explain details of many nursing procedures just to calm him down.

Once, when he needed to use a commode, a nurse peeked through the curtains and he yelled, 'Rape!!' He wanted to discharge himself; I had to explain to him that there was treatment for him in the hospital that would help him.

He wanted to pay for his hospitalisation and we had to reassure him that was the NHS, no one had to pay. He wanted to smoke and drink alcohol and of course he was not allowed to. In the last twenty years living in England, he seemed to have lived a totally Chinese life, and had rarely moved outside the Chinese community. The western world was completely alien to him.

In hospital, Chan could not eat English food and his wife had to bring him his own food. But the strong and unique smell of his salt fish and pork drove the nurses away. But he was getting used to sleeping on the ward; he had a kind nature and eventually got on well with the nurses. Somehow he survived five weeks in the hospital.

After his discharge, several times he cooked some delicious food and took it to the ward to treat the staff.

Tale 8

In court – 1988

'Gung ho, work together'
A Chinese proverb.

In 1987, I was appointed as an Assistant Director of Nursing at Burton-upon-Trent. One of my responsibilities was in charge of Burton general hospital. The hospital does not exist anymore because it was closed when the new Queen's Hospital opened. The old hospital has since been demolished and many houses have been built on the site.

I was responsible for eleven wards, all acute wards—both medical and surgical, an ear, nose and throat ward and an emergency admission unit. The ophthalmic ward was situated by a main road, on the first floor. The patients were mostly elderly and stayed a short time on the ward. There was complaint that at nights, the chip shop opposite stayed open till after midnight and noises made by the customers disturbed the patients sleep.

The night nursing officer complained to the shop but to no avail. The Head of Nursing was informed and the result was fruitless. The chip shop was supposed to be closed at midnight but it did not stick to the rules because it got a lot of good business after midnight. The Police did not seem to have the power either. Nurses seemed to have accepted that was a difficult situation to handle. Many patients did not complain because they were mostly short stayed patients and they just put up with the noise.

One day, I was handed a letter from the Community Health Council (CHC). An ex-patient has written a letter of complaint to the CHC which was representative of the public, showing concern about the noise and hence the well beings of the patients. I was asked to go along with a lady called Jean from CHC over the weekend, starting at before midnight till one in the morning to monitor the activities of the chip shop.

I could not refuse the offer. It seemed Jean had already co-operated with the Police.

I accompanied Jean for the long weekend and recorded our findings. It was not a surprise to me to note the chip shop did open till one in the morning.

Although it was a tiring exercise, it was rewarding. Three months later, I was asked to attend a court hearing at Stafford. I have never been to a court before. And I had no advice from my seniors and I just had to report what I saw. Fortunately, I did a full report of the findings for the weekend and I had my copy in hand.

The proceedings were like what we saw on television. A policeman, Jean and I were summoned to the stand and we gave our versions of the findings of the weekend. We all reported the same and confirmed that the shop should have been closed at midnight but it did not shut till one in the morning because of the brisk business. The noise did disturb the patients on the ophthalmic ward and they had complained. The owner of the shop admitted to the breaking the rule of closing times. He was fined and said he would obey the rules in the future. If not, he might have to go to prison.

On reflection, it was amazing to note that we had to rely on an outside body, the Community Health Council, to take action and to take the owner to court so that the shop owner would obey the law.

Tale 9

Bid for equipment in the hospital – 1989

'And money is like muck, not good except it be spread'
Francis Bacon

When I was a senior nurse in the Burton Hospitals, occasionally we were asked what equipment we might need on the wards. The ward sisters usually smiled and told me. Their faces told me that they knew that the chances of getting that piece of equipment would be remote because the money was always not there. We had to somehow manage to get things or equipment on the wards. We had to manage with what we had.

One day my boss, the Director of Nursing Services, asked if I could go in place of him to a big meeting with many medical consultants to bid some equipment. It was a few weeks before the end of the financial year (that was April of the year) and not all the money had been spent. Jack, the director, said to me, 'Patrick, it might be a waste of your time; we don't always get anything from this meeting, although we have £250,000 left to spend.'

'Really, 'I replied. 'But we need three resuscitation trolleys; ours are so old and we need newer suction machines for when patients come back from operating theatre. It is quite urgent, you know.'

'Well, some consultants would say the children warrant more money and the cardiac doctors have their needs too.'

'Okay' I sounded disappointed.

'You will soon know. It will be good experience for you. I shall have a word with the medical director; we might have a chance to get one resus trolley, if we are lucky. Don't be too disappointed if we do not get any.'

'Okay.'

*

The evening meeting started at 18.00. I have never seen so many medical consultants in a room at one time. There were many specialty surgeons, orthopaedics, general surgeons, eye and ear and nose and throat consultants, gynaecologists, physicians and paediatricians, just to name a few. All wanted more equipment for their own specialties. I thought that my nursing colleague from operating theatres had much better a chance to get pieces of equipment than me. What was more important? Without a piece of vital equipment in the operating theatre, one could not operate efficiently. But how could we about without the new resus trolley on the ward?

The General Manager and Medical Director started the meeting by spelling out the money that the hospital had left and it certainly sounded a lot. But with the medical equipment costing so much money, the hospital could only afford one page of the equipment requests out of five pages of the demand. The nursing equipment was on the fourth page. We had a remote chance of getting any new equipment.

The presentation started and one could see the united front of some consultants, uniting and supporting each other so that they both could win their bids. It was no surprise that they were from the children's and cardiac departments because from the newspaper exposure, the public always supported children and patients with heart problems. The general surgeons complained about their situations of never getting any more funding for better equipment for their departments.

One surgeon threatened to tell the local newspaper that the equipment used in the theatre was obsolete and would be harmful to patients. The fellow surgeons supported each other and at the end, they were pleased that they had bid successfully for some equipment. Then my colleague from the operating theatre explained that his equipment was so old and out-of –date and he was supported well by many surgeons. He was relieved to know he got most of what he wanted. All these pieces of equipments were so expensive that the money nearly ran out after half an hour of discussion. Jack, my boss, was right. When it came to my turn to support the bid for ward equipment, there was not much money left. Our priority was low on the wish list. I replied that it was not fair that nurses always did poorly at these meetings. There was a stunned silence amongst the senior doctors. But through a long discussion, we were granted money to have a new resuscitation trolley. I smiled wryly. One out of three, big deal!

No wonder all ward sisters bought their equipment from the ward funds donated by some grateful patients from their own wards, some after their deaths. In a hospital, there was just not enough money to go round to buy new equipment. One would say that it should be the hospital's responsibilities to purchase good equipment for patients. But the truth was that there were always a budget and a panel to agree on buying the equipment. And we did rely heavily on charity and fundraising to buy nursing equipment.

There was no fairness in this distribution of funds. What was more important? To buy a piece of equipment for the heart patients or for general surgical patients? It was hard to decide. But the public influence was paramount to influence decisions. One ear specialist consultant commented that there has been so much progress in eye surgery because of the public perception of the fact that it was sad and horrible to see people who were blind or could not see well and hence there has been so much public support and funding. The surgery for cataracts or for glaucoma has improved by leaps and bounds in the last twenty years.

Yet in ear surgery, there has been hardly any progress at all. The last piece of funding for ear research was in the sixties when astronauts returned back from the moon and there were problems with their ears. Since the publicity was not there, there was not much support and funding for any research.

Tale 10

Busiest day on the ward – 1977

'They say hard work never hurt anybody,
but I figure why take a chance.'
Ronald Reagan.

I was dreading going to work on this Wednesday morning. I knew that when I arrived on the acute medical ward, there would be only one member of staff on duty with me, auxiliary nurse (a/x) Preston because the others were all off sick with tonsillitis, and diarrhoea. I informed Nursing Officer Helen and she told that she was not sure she could get me help from elsewhere.

When she saw me in the morning, I was trying to sort out breakfast for twenty-two patients with a/x Preston. We did it as quickly as we could and then we both were feeding two patients who were too ill to feed themselves. We did not say much to Nursing Officer Helen and she left the wards quickly to find help.

Helen managed to find two other auxiliary nurses to help us. Normally, we needed six members of staff on duty to do a reasonable job of giving good care. Now we had four and I was the only trained nurse on duty. I suggested to Helen that the patients would not have a bed bath or a general bath this morning because we had not enough staff. She agreed that we would just give them a wash. If the whole hospital had not had sufficient staff to manage the care, what else could we do?

I went round and greeted all patients to ensure they had reasonable nights' sleep and that they were all content. I ensured all the charts were in order, fluid charts and charts for temperature, pulse and respirations.

I started the drug round at 8.45, a bit earlier than usual; knowing the drug round would take at least two hours because of the constant interruptions for giving answers to relatives and doctors. In addition, I was expecting three ward rounds, one from a registrar and two from the consultants.

I quickly checked the two patients with intravenous infusions running on time and their fluid balance charts were filled in properly because the doctors were very likely to check them.

The registrar knew that I did not have a full quota of staff and we did the ward round speedily, discharging two patients so that we could admit two new ones in the afternoon.

I stopped the drug round temporarily at 9.30 because one consultant wanted to do his usual round. I could not postpone that because it concerned patients' treatment. The ward round took twenty minutes and there were drugs to change and I had to order them from the pharmacy. As I restarted the drug round, I was needed on the phone. Mike, the houseman, apologized because he knew that I was busy but informed me that there was a patient with chest pain to be admitted from the emergency admission unit.

I took a deep breathe and thought to myself, 'It is going to be a busy and lousy day.' I had to leave the only dressing to be done for the afternoon staff because they would be two trained nurses on duty on a late shift. Fortunately, Nursing Officer Helen learnt about my emergency admission and offered to finish off the drug round for me. I thanked her sincerely for the help.

Just after I said my thanks, I saw a surgical consultant Mr. Fish walking into the ward.

'Hello, I have been asked to see a Mr. Smith with some abdominal problem.' He said.

'Sure, this way.' I was expecting a surgeon to see the patient but normally he came in the afternoon. I drew the curtain to ensure privacy and luckily, Mr. Smith was in his bed. The surgeon palpated the abdomen and thought for a while. Mr. Fish turned to me and said, 'Has he just had his breakfast?'

'Yes.'

'Okay. From now on, nil by mouth please. He is for this afternoon's list, a laporatomy and then he will go to the surgical ward, okay.' I nodded.

Mr. Fish explained what was to happen to the patient's situation and Mr. Smith agreed.

'Mr. Poon, I shall ask my houseman to come to sign a consent form with him, okay.'

'Okay.' I thought to myself, 'I better ask Preston to shave him soon too, a preparation before the operation.'

I was getting the bed ready for the emergency patient with chest pain and Nursing Officer Helen saw me working busily and she suggested, 'I know that you have been working non-stop. I think that you should leave the ward and have a break, Patrick.'

I thanked Helen for her consideration. At the canteen, I had my usual cup of tea and toasts, relishing the quiet moment. Ward Sister Holly was leaving the canteen and sat by my table.

'So you have been busy, Patrick?'

'Yes, can I ask you why you want to work on the busiest ward in the hospital?'

'Well, it is not like that all the time.' I replied. 'And it is good experience.'

'You can say that. But let me tell you, news travels fast here in the hospital. And you are getting a good reputation.'

I was so pleased to hear that.

'Good luck, Patrick.'

'Thanks.'

I went back to the ward after a ten minute break. I thought I needed to go back to see the new patient who had arrived and I was right. He was a young man in his thirties, with lots of chest pain. I was helping the nurse to lift him onto the bed.

'I think that he will need some more morphine for the pain, Patrick.' The emergency admission nurse has suggested. I went quickly to check with Helen in the office. 10 mgms of morphine, a good strong analgesic, I thought. Helen came with me and I injected into his buttock. The patient, John, was trying to relax and then he just collapsed. Froth came from his mouth and his eyes rolled up.

'Cardiac arrest!' I shouted and started thumping onto his sternum. Helen was trying to lay the patient flat. She also tried to remove the headrest of the bed to make room for the cardiac team to intubate the patient. A/X Preston saw us and dialed the internal telephone number 333 instantly, alerting the cardiac arrest team. Preston also wheeled the ward emergency trolley by the bed.

Fortunately the coronary care unit (CCU) was very near our acute medical ward and the team arrived speedily. A house doctor tried to suck out the mouth secretion with the suction machine and then to intubate the patient and he succeeded and connected the tube to a machine, helping the patient to breathe.

A CCU nurse took over from me to continue to thumb his sternum. Another doctor connected the machine onto the electric pad and ordered, 'Do not touch the bed.' We all followed the instruction and the fibrillation worked. John's heart pattern was flat but then after the electric shock, he was back to normal sinus rhythm.

'Good.' One doctor said, 'Let's transfer the patient next door to CCU.'

In due course, Helen was trying to console and explain the situation to the patient's wife. Thank goodness Helen was there to help but if only the patient had not admitted to my ward, all these could be done in the CCU. Now, I had to write and record what happened in detail and then clean our resuscitation trolley and replace all items used. It was not to be my day.

A/X Preston was very good and experienced and she made tea for the relative and also wanted to ensure all the basic work was done, with the help from the other two auxiliary nurses from other wards.. She did a marvelous job in helping me.

'Patrick, I am not going off at 1 pm. I will stay longer to help you. You need more help' she volunteered.

'Thanks you very much Press (nicknamed for Preston, as we all called her). I will make sure Helen will pay you extra hour. Press nodded and smiled. She started serving lunch for me on the ward as I was clearing up the chaos of the procedure and equipment used during the process. I tried to write as quickly as I could so that I could hand over the records and paperwork for the CCU.

I was in the office, writing my report and the telephone rang.

'Charge Nurse Poon speaking.' I answered the phone.

'Hello Patrick, sorry to trouble you. It is Mrs. Brown, 'I don't know why my husband just rang me from your ward, and He cannot find his false teeth.'

'Oh.' I was speechless.

'Could you find it for me please?'

'Of course.' I put the phone down. I saw Press walking by and I told him about Mr. Brown's missing false teeth. Both of us shrugged and looked up the sky. Press went searching though Mr. Brown's locker and pyjamas and eventually found the false teeth in his pyjamas top pocket, wrapped in tissues. I asked Press to ring and relayed the good news to Mrs. Brown.

The faces of the nurses on the late shift were arriving and I felt more relieved because they knew the ward very well to get on with the work on the ward.

AX Preston peeped through the door in the office and said, 'Patrick, I know that you have been working non stop and we have saved you a lunch.'

'Bless you.' I said thankfully.

Then I went to the ward to thank all the auxiliary nurses from the other wards who had helped us. They had done a good job by ensuring the patients were fed, cleaned and were fairly happy. I did wish I had more staff to look after them better.

With many events happening this morning, it took me forty five minutes to give the report to the nurses on a late shift. With no time for a proper lunch in the canteen, I gulped down my lunch in the kitchen in ten minutes and then I started to write the ward report. But my hopes of having a quieter afternoon were crashed when the telephone rang.

We had to admit two new patients with breathing problems,

one with asthma and one with long history of bronchitis. As we had no empty beds, we had to inform two patients that they had to be transferred to another ward in a convalescent hospital nearby. Then the houseman from outpatients wanted to bring a patient down from the clinic for venesection--a procedure to drain blood from a patient because he had too many red blood cells. I explained to the doctor that we had had a very busy day and asked if the patient could come to the ward the next day for the procedure. Fortunately, the doctor was co-operative.

I went into the coronary care unit to see the patient I'd had on the ward in the morning. Fortunately he was recovering. He was a lucky man who was in the right place in the right time when he cardiac arrested and we brought him back to life.

The nurse on the late shift said that I ought to write the report on all the patients. I went to the office with a cup of tea. It took me forty five minutes. Because I had another trained nurse on with me, I was interrupted less than in the morning. The trained nurse could get on with doing the afternoon drug rounds and the dressing. She checked that our fluid charts were up-to-date and the intravenous infusions were on schedule.

'It is after 5 pm, Patrick, you ought to go home.' My only trained nurse said. I looked at my watch; it was after half-past five in the afternoon. I knew that Nursing Officer Helen has gone home.

'You will be okay then?' I asked the trained nurse.

'You have done more than your share today.' She said. I felt that I had. As I was walking towards my car, I felt that I had a sense of relief and also an achievement. It has been a very busy day and somewhat rewarding. We have given best possible care and the patients told me that they were fine.

I took off my white coat before I went in the car and

noticed the dark blue appellate of my charge nurse uniform. It was a responsible post, even at my age of twenty-seven; I felt good and headed home.

Tale 11

Damien, a patient with a prolonged erection of the penis – 1982

'Clayton ward, Charge nurse speaking.'

'Hello Patrick, it's Mike. I am in the emergency admission room.'

'Are you okay, Mike?' Mike was my houseman, junior surgical doctor on call.

'Well, got an admission for you, I'm afraid that he wants you to admit him.'

'Oh, how so? I have some good nurses on with me.'

'The patient wants a male nurse to admit him.'

'Right.' I was inquisitive.

'This is a young man, thirty-two years old and he has an erection of his penis.'

'Tell me more.'

'He has been erect for four hours and he will feel embarrassed to be admitted by a female nurse.'

'Okay, what happened?'

'He was making love in the afternoon, twice, successfully but it is still up.'

'Lucky him. Sorry, I was jesting. Must be uncomfortable.'

'Right. He is very concerned and he is feeling sore. I have not seen such case before.'

'Nor me.' I confessed.

'Nor the registrar nor the senior houseman.'

'Okay, let's admit him and I do appreciate that he is sensitive about it.'

When I informed the other nurses, all of them female, they all giggled but did not want to admit this new patient either. I prepared a bed for him with all the relevant charts and a cradle.

The young man was brought onto my ward on a trolley. All female nurses had a look at him and admired his good looks but went to do some other tasks. He moved himself onto the bed quite well but his face looked red with embarrassment. I put a cradle to lessen the pressure on his sensitive part. He appreciated the help and answered all the personal details like name and address.

His name was Damien. He had no family history with such ailment and he was feeling sore and it was his first time of his experiencing this unfortunate episode.

The surgical registrar rang the urologist consultant on call. Mr. Major was a progressive surgeon and had been in post for one year. His treatment and care to his patients was dynamic but he was also perplexed by the situation. He did not think that he should operate but should treat the patient conservatively.

Fortunately, he was in the coffee room with five other consultants. They discussed Damien's case with interest. It seemed that none of the doctors had treated a patient with this problem but one consultant had heard of a case like it.

Mike was instructed by Mr. Major to sedate the patient by prescribing valium orally and then pethidine, a painkiller, by injection. Mike also was asked to put up an intravenous infusion with heparin. Mike was told that Damien might have a blood disorder, maybe some blood clotting defect. Heparin is an anti-coagulant drug with its aim to thin the blood. Damien's girlfriend was with him but he had not told his parents.

I was glad to have admitted Damien rather than a female nurse.

Mr. Major was very kind and came to the ward to see the patient. He was professional and did not look at the illness as a joke. He talked to Damien, just to ensure his history was the same as he was told by his registrar. Damien was pleased the senior doctor had been to see him and he was reassured that he would be okay in future. He was very relieved.

The mixture of the medications and treatment took six hours to work and Damien's erection had subsided much to his delight. But he was still worried. His blood clotting mechanism was abnormal and he was referred to a haematologist. Damien was kept for another day on the ward and he was okay. The urologist consultant came to see him and explained the possible causes of his illness. He was discharged under the care of the haematologist.

Tale 12

Patients with arterial diseases – 1971 and 1983

'I feel a feeling which I feel you all feel.'
A sermon.

In nursing, there were always patients one came across that one would never forget either for the good or bad. I remember one such patient many years ago by the name of Charles Dickens.

That was at Newmarket General Hospital in 1971. Charles Dickens was a small man, thin and drawn, with no limbs. He had an artificial arm attached to his elbow, like a bionic man. He was from Newmarket and suffered from Buerger's disease.

Buerger's disease causes inflammation of blood vessels in legs and arms, particularly in hands and feet. It leads to narrowing and blockage of the blood vessels so that blood flow to hands and feet is reduced. This causes pain and other symptoms and may eventually lead to damage and death of the tissues in hands and/or feet.

The exact cause is not known but it affects smokers more. The single most important thing you can do if you are diagnosed with Buerger's disease is to stop smoking. This can help to stop the disease from getting worse and reduces your chance of needing surgical removal of a finger, a toe, or worse.

Charles Dickens had been a heavy smoker for most of his life. He knew that he must not smoke but he always gave in, despite the risks he was taking. He now had with a suspected bowel obstruction. One wondered how he could continue smoking; especially he was losing one limb at a time. Nicotine obviously meant more to him than his limbs.

However, he was still smoking with the help of his artificial hand and arm. Nurses had to wash him, toilet him and feed him. However, he was still however, cheerful.

The Government supported him by giving him benefits and spent thousands of pounds on the operations he had. The good old National Health Service footed the bills. One wonders if other countries would provide such a service.

The whole nursing and medical team talked about him. They also knew, because of his immobility, his bowel movement would be limited and hence, intestinal obstruction could be expected. I was on the surgical ward for six weeks and we looked after him before and after his operation. He had his bowel obstruction removed and was recovering from the operation well. He was on the ward for the six weeks I was there in my allocation. I heard that he was discharged home eventually and he was still smoking. Now, with his limited quality of life, his only enjoyment was inhaling his nicotine.

*

Some twelve years later, I became a senior charge nurse of an acute surgical ward. Arterial surgery was one of our specialties. We had arterial surgery performed by Mr. Fish, an efficient arterial surgeon. He operated every Thursday morning and usually one operation took four hours, a whole morning to save a man's leg. The operation could be obliterating some arterial of the arteries, or doing a transplant graft. (To take a good piece of vein and invert it upside down and graft it to the diseased part of the artery-the reason for inverting the vein was veins had valves hindering the blood flow and if one inverted it, it could function as an artery.) On Thursday afternoon, I normally put an extra nurse on duty, to 'special' or focus the nursing care just on this patient, after his big operation. This was in the days of before intensive care was thought of.

The duty of this nurse was to take the blood pressure and the pulse of the patent every fifteen minutes and observe the site of the operation closely, in case it bled. A fall in blood pressure and a consistent rise in pulse was an indication of internal hemorrhage. A cradle would be used to lessen the pressure of blankets onto the wound.

Before such a big operation, patients had to have an arteriogramme done to confirm the blockage of the arteries which were usually in the legs. We had countless patients for arteriogramme every week. The cause of the arterial disease was due to artheroma blocking the arteries or Beurger's disease. The latter was uncommon but the former was common. Narrowing of the arteries was common and artheroma was mainly caused by eating food rich in cholesterols such as cream cakes or fatty meat.

We remember Derek, a former patient very well. He had the arteriogrammes done three times because he was allergic to the dye. During the arteriogram, a white dye was injected into the arteries so x rays could be done to confirm any blockage of arteries. The third time was successful for Derek because the X-ray department used a different form of dye for the procedure and it confirmed his blockage in need of an operation. He was on the waiting list which was five months.

One Saturday afternoon, Derek was admitted as an emergency because he had severe pain down his legs. The surgical doctors saw him and reckoned that his femoral artery was nearly completely blocked. This warranted an urgent operation; otherwise he would loose his legs quickly.

On admission, Derek was in surgical shock in severe pain, looking very pale and clammy. He was on oxygen and we gave him a morphine injection to ease the pain. He was starved nil by mouth for four hours and was surgically shaved, ready for the operation. Derek and I hardly had time for any social chat. Mr. Fish came in to operate and it took the normal four hours in the evening.

Post-operatively, Derek recovered reasonable well and looked better. Routinely, nurses monitored his blood pressure and pulse every fifteen minutes to start with and later half hourly. The main reason was to detect any internal bleeding. A fall in blood pressure and an increase in pulse was the main indication. House doctors and registrar came more regularly to see him too. We gave him strong analgesics to alleviate the pain.

He had a reasonable sleep during the night. The wound site was satisfactory, with no sign of bleeding. There was a slight swelling and doctors saw it. There was a slight increase in pulse and fall in blood pressure which I was not too happy with. Doctors were informed but they wanted to wait and see. The houseman told the registered surgeon and both doctors wanted to sit on it and to wait.

Something bothered me and I was not sure what. Derek was not mentally the same though the observation of pulse and blood pressure was not too bad. This went on for nearly two hours on the Sunday morning. Doctors were informed but they took little of my concern.

I did something that I did not do often. In fact, it was only the second time I had done it. I rang Mr. Fish, the consultant at home. He was nice and did not mind me ringing him. I told him of my concern. We had worked together for two years and got on well.

Mr. Fish came in to see the patient, telling the junior doctors that he was nearby the ward, seeing another patient and hence he thought he came in to see how Derek was doing. I was glad to note that he felt the same that Derek was not his usual self, remembering that he and I had met Derek many times before. Mr. Fish removed the dressing on the wound and discovered a swelling that might indicate some form of bleeding. He decided to take Derek to the operating theatre again.

On the operating table, Mr. Fish found that Derek was bleeding internally. I was pleased that I had made the decision to contact the consultant. Derek's bleeding was stopped and the wound was sutured with stronger catgut.

It was pleasing to see Derek was starting to recover well and he started to behave normally again. He was on the road of recovery.

Mr. Fish came to the ward personally to tell me the findings in the operation and thanked me for the concern. We shook hands and he smiled wryly.

Many consultants told us before that ward sisters and charge nurses worked permanently on the wards and we knew more about the patients than the houseman and registrars who came and went every few months. It was nice to feel respected by the senior doctors. In fact, I remember very well that when I left the surgical ward to become a nursing officer of a surgical unit, two consultants told me that they wished I stayed on the ward to work because they told me I was a good charge nurse. These words meant a lot to me and I did not forget these kind words of praise.

I enjoyed my five years as charge nurse on the acute medical and surgical wards. The excitement, the satisfaction and the hard work was stimulating and rewarding. I had to make quick decisions and I was working with dedicated nurses and doctors. It was a fantastic phase of my life.

12A

The Tree

I think I shall never see,
words I write as lovely as a tree.
Words are written by a fool like me,
but only the Good Lord can create a tree.

I remember the trees up the Heath,
it stands as lonesome as they can be,
Through the rain and the wind, it stands there,
through the joy, the happiness and the nightmare.

But how about the tress at Lantao Island,
standing there so still and forlorn.
And the maple trees stand tall in Canada,
as red and magnificent as they all matter.

In the busy city of Hong Kong,
there are trees amongst the tall buildings.
The birds live there amongst its chattering.
Their singings wake me up from my dream,
but I do not mind as I feel so serene.

And the oak trees, elm trees and the maple trees,
you are everywhere for me to see.
The trees are like my old friend, the sea.
if you are not there, I will miss thee.

Patrick K S Poon.
May, 2013.

Year 1990s

Tale 13

The twelve hour shift

'Time brings all things to pass'
Aeschylus

The off duty of the twelve hours shift is quite common in psychiatric nursing in the UK. The main reason is shortage of staff. Usually the staff would work from eight in the morning to eight in the evening. In mental nursing, the physical demand is not great but the emotional strain is. Fulltime nurses or carers would work three days, twelve hours shifts that are called long days and they would have four days off a week to compensate.

In general nursing, long days are not practised much. Probably, it is because it is so physically demanding. In the 1960's and the 1970's, we had to do split shifts, that is, working from 7.30-14.00 and to take 14.00-17.00 off and back to work 17.00-21.00.; quite a long day for us and it was cheaper way of using labour workforce for the hospital.

From the 1980s, the split shifts seemed to be disappearing, mainly because the afternoon work was just as busy as during the mornings and evenings and certain number of nurses were needed. But we seldom did have to work long days at all. Hence, working long days were new to me.

When I first worked in a nursing home in 1997, I had to

work few long days. It was a different situation, in that there were just not many carers to change the shifts with. I tried it once or twice and it was not too bad but it was mentally taxing.

In the nursing home, the basic nursing care was done by the carers and the trained nurse's duties were to administer drugs, do dressings and various nursing tasks. We were there to advise the well-brings of the residents. If needed, we called the general practitioners. When one started at eight in the morning, one would be mentally tired by 17.30 and wished that one was at home, relaxing. Not many nurses enjoyed the long days of work, especially if the nurse was likely to be working on his own and very often he was the only trained nurse on duty in the care home. Having a registered nurse on duty was a requirement at the nursing home as it was under the control of the Health Authority.

I once did a long day and an early shift the following day of eight in the morning till four in the afternoon. When one o'clock came on that day, I was told that the trained nurse in the evening was off sick. She was the only trained nurse on duty. Ringing the Nursing Agency and asking for a trained nurse as a replacement was a chore and after two hours of ringing, it was in vain. Getting a trained nurse in an emergency was not an easy task. All the bank nurses of the home could not work either because of the short notice. I was tired out and did not want to work that evening.

What could I do? By the Nursing Code of Standard, trained nurses could not leave the shift unless she/he has handed over to another trained nurse. So I was stuck. The only nurse available was an enrolled nurse. She was not supposed to be in charge, unless in an emergency. Normally, registered nurses were in charge of the shift.

If I was working in a hospital, there would be more flexibility. Help could be had from other wards. In the nursing home, a trained nurse could feel so much alone.

I rang the Health Authority which was responsible for nursing home problems. I explained that I did a long day the day before and now I was exhausted and did not wish to work another long day. I explained that I had no help from any nurses or from nursing agencies. The only possible help was from the enrolled nurse.

The Senior nurse from the Health Authority on the phone was thinking. I explained further that if I stayed on to work another long day and made a nursing mistake, I would not be accountable. The Senior Nurse from the Health Authority relented and I had at last avoided doing another long day.

In the world of medicine, working twelve hours shift is common. Certainly, it happened frequently in the 1980s and 1990s. Junior doctors, especially houseman (just qualified doctors) would work from Friday and the weekend as well, day and on night duties. Above the grade, there was usually a registered doctor on duty as well.

I was a charge nurse on the ward then. One of my responsibilities was to ensure patients' care was good.

Very often, I was worried about the well-being of junior doctors. At times, they had no time to eat because of continuous emergencies. It was common that some of them had not slept for one night or even two. Ward sister like me reported this to the senior doctors so that they knew the junior doctors were not functioning properly.

A friend of mine was a house surgeon and he once had no sleep for two days and two nights. Fortunately, the registered surgeon noticed that he was asleep holding a retractor during an operation because he was so tired. It was a relief when I learnt that he was sent home to rest.

Unfortunately, many consultants were not sympathetic. 'Well, Patrick, we have done it before, now it is their turn.' was their answer. No mention of care about their performance in treating patients then! Fortunately, this was brought up for the meetings at the British Medical Association; junior doctors now have a better deal than many years ago.

*

A good friend of mine was a trained midwife and a home birth specialist. She was called Becky and her story of working shifts was scarier. Doing home birth was her pride and joy and she gained great satisfaction from them. Also it was better for the patients. She was accountable for a group of pregnant ladies and most preferred a home birth.

She was doing a late shift of 13.00-21.00 and the workload was heavy and demanding, like most of the duties in the NHS. Then a call came at 19.00, saying one of her home births was contracting and was asking for help. Becky was the midwife and went to help. She stayed in the woman's home all night, observing but the baby did not come till seven the following morning.

The procedure took another two hours and the mother and family and Becky were delighted with the outcome though it took some hours. Becky never had any rest from 13.00 the previous day and much sleep all night. Because of the emergency, her boss could not find any midwife to relieve her either, so the exhausted Becky had to start the clinic duties in the morning and work till four in the afternoon. Her husband was very angry with the situation and threatened to ring to complain to her boss. But Becky said that it was the same with all midwives and so did not want any trouble. The husband did not want to upset the wife and did not ring.

At four in the afternoon the following day, some more than twenty four hours later, Becky had to drive forty minutes to get home. She opened the car windows so the cold wind would keep her awake. As she was driving the A38, she fell asleep. Suddenly, a strong hand woke her up. She realised that she has been to sleep and was upset. She looked around but there was no one in the car. Who else could it be? Beck was too exhausted to care. She stopped in a lay by and fell asleep for thirty minutes before she drove home safely. Becky called the mysterious figure her guardian angel.

It seemed that when Becky told others the tale, other midwives have experienced the similar situations. But Becky's boss never believed her and the same care in the maternity services continued.

Tale 14

Ward sisters

'Memory is the mother of wisdom.'

1 Sister Bluntie Rigsby – 1973

I was a third year student nurse and working on a male surgical ward at Kettering General Hospital. I was on a rotation plan in order to gain a variety of experience. Sister Rigsby was the senior sister on the male surgical ward. She was a small lady who wore glasses, and was in her fifties. She was an old fashioned type of ward sister, demanding hard work and discipline. If you did not do the work, you would be in trouble. Like many ward sisters in those days, she was a spinster and devoted her life to nursing.

Her manner was sharp to male patients and staff, hence gaining a nickname of Bluntie. However, many people did say that she was fair. In our male nurses' home, male student nurses gossiped and thought she was okay and fair, as long as you worked. Some did even say she liked male nurses better. She did not like female nurses gossiping nor giggling. Some young student nurses did not like her because they thought that she was old-fashioned and had too much discipline. I was quite apprehensive at the thought of going to go there to work.

The doctors and surgical consultants respected her as the leader of the ward. Young housemen had to behave and work hard otherwise they would get reported to the consultants. The consultants liked her because she ran a very tight ship and so the standard of care was high.

The junior sister was a much younger lady, also small in stature but quietly efficient. On the ward, I gained good experience in doing dressings and pre-operative and post operative care of surgical patients. I just did what I was supposed to do as a student nurse and always tried to show that I was keen on working and learning. I did lots of pre-operative care such as surgical shaves, using suppositories and general bathing to ensure the patients were clean. Post operatively, I was asked to prepare lots of inhalations for patients to help them with their breathing.

Some female students were in trouble and were reduced to tears by Bluntie for wearing too much make-up or having long finger nails. One was told off for flirting too much with the male patients. A professional was the order of the day. Sister Rigsby said no one was allowed to whistle on the ward because it was not professional. In my heart, I know she was correct.

After three weeks the college of Nursing informed the ward that I ought to have my assessment there. I froze because I had to be assessed by Sister Rigsby. I assumed that she must be a tough assessor. However, when she talked to me in her office, she was quite pleasant though very old fashioned and formal. She always called me Nurse Poon.

I sat down quietly in the office and she told me that she thought I had settled down on the ward well and thought that I should attempt doing my assessment there. In those days, I was quiet and just got on with my work. I was pleased with her comment.

In those days, student nurses had to pass four clinical assessments: doing a drug round, an aseptic technique (doing a dressing effectively), a total patient's care in a shift and running the ward for one day. I had already passed the first three assessments but the fourth was the toughest. Sister Rigsby said that I could observe her running the ward and learn from her and then I could have one trial run and then be assessed by her. I was not in a position to refuse and it did seem reasonable.

During the time I observed her running the ward, she taught me how to prepare ward rounds with the doctors, what to prepare: always check the blood results if they were normal and ensure recent x-rays were available and case notes ready for patients going to the operating theatre. She emphasized that pre-medication for patients before operations must be done precisely so that patients could be really relaxed. I would see that all these nursing procedures must be effectively run for the best care of the patients.

I followed her on doctors' ward rounds and I noticed that she was so experienced and knew all the patients' care and treatments. A very good aspect of working with her was that she always made sure the staff had proper tea breaks and time off for lunch. She was a professional and took things very seriously. Patients liked her because she was proper and clear in her instructions though she was a stickler in discipline.

On the day of the assessment, I arrived on the ward at 7.00 instead of 7.30, wanting to know more about the ward activities so that I could be more in control. We had our normal quota of staff, six of us on duty. It was going to be a routine busy day, operations in the morning, routine admissions for the operating theatre list tomorrow and dressings and medication to be done.

Sister Rigsby arrived promptly on the ward and had her usual cup of tea. She seemed pleased with my allocation of staff to do the tasks of the day. Two members of the staff were allocated to help washing patients and to sit them up in a chair. One was doing the dressings and inhalations. Another nurse was taking patients to theatre and then back again.

We had three operations that morning. Two were for repair of inguinal hernia and one cholecystectomy, the removal of the gall bladder.

I went around the patients and greeted them all and tried to find out if there had been problems during the night. There was none. Was it calm before the storm?

I checked the pre-medication with Sister Rigsby for two patients before their operations and two other nurses were doing breakfast for the patients. On the surgical ward, there were not usually many breakfasts to do because some patients were due for operations, hence they were not allowed to eat and some patients had just had an operation the previous day and thus not allowed to eat too much.

The registrar soon came on duty at 8.15 and did a fast ward round to check for any problems; they were none. We also chatted to see who could be discharged so that beds could be made available for new patients to be admitted in the afternoon.

Then I did the drug round before 9.00. Sister Rigsby helped and even took a patient to the operating theatre. I was relieved to see she was in a good mood. At 9.30, I was told that an emergency patient would be admitted suffering with appendicitis and would go to theatre in the afternoon.

Appendicitis was the commonest emergency admissions on a surgical ward. There were no other nurses available so I thought I would prepare the bed and admit the patient and also surgically prepare him. The storm had started, I thought.

I was right. The student nurse who was allocated by me to do the dressings came and asked me to look at the dressing she was doing. Something was wrong, she said. Sister Rigsby and I looked at each other and went behind the curtain. The patient was an obese man, recovering from a cholecystectomy. He was coughing and felt something had come out. The nurse took off the dressing and it seemed something resembling a part of the gut was there. I had never seen this sort of thing before and I was sweating and thinking quickly what to do. Sister Rigsby was looking at me to make a decision.

I remembered reading once a surgical complication could be a burst abdomen. I wondered this was what I was observing. I reassured the patient and said that I would inform a doctor. Instinctively, I went to fetch a solution of normal saline and a large dressing pad. I put on a pair of gloves and put it on the nurses' dressing trolley. I soaked the dressing pad in saline and put in on the patient's wound. I secured the dressing with a firm tape, trying to apply some pressure.

The houseman was contacted and he came to the ward straight away. Sister Rigsby followed me wherever I went. I explained to sister that I had never seen such a situation and was not sure if I was doing right. She smiled for the first time of my seven weeks' stay on the ward and told me it was the correct procedure. It was a burst abdomen. She could see I was nervous and sweating and she reassured me I was doing okay. She asked what else I could do with the patient. I said that I would ensure the patient's relative was informed and the consent form would be signed by the patient.

The doctor came back and told me to starve the patient with the burst abdomen and he would be at the end of the morning operating list. The theatre rang then and asked if I could send a nurse to fetch a patient back following his operation. I looked around and there was no nurse available, everyone was busy. I asked Sister Rigsby if I could go to theatre. She said not as I was in charge of the ward but she herself would go to fetch the patent back from theatre.

Then the nurse who was washing some patients came to report that an old patient had fallen over but that he had not hurt himself. I went to see the patient but he was fine. I asked the nurse if she could write the incident up in the accident book. I told her that I would inform the doctor and also the relative later on.

The emergency patient with the acute appendicitis arrived and I admitted him and prepared him for theatre. The unexpected emergency patient and the event of the burst abdomen and the fall interrupted the smooth pattern of our work. Fortunately, the patients were all okay.

The dressings and coffee rounds were done and, we were not very far behind in the ward schedule. In due course, Sister Rigsby and I checked and gave two post operative injections to relieve the patients' pain.

Lunch arrived and we did it satisfactorily. On a surgical ward not many patients were allowed to eat fully so this was done quickly and smoothly. Then the afternoon staff arrived and I felt relieved that half a day was done. Everything had been so busy but I felt sure that I had made no mistakes.

The afternoon staff arrived for the late shift and one of these was the junior sister. |She was quiet and a very good experienced worker. Before the report I went round all the patients to ensure they were okay and checked that all the fluid and temperature charts.

I gave a full report to all the staff with Sister Rigsby at my side, observing me. I reported fully to the staff and felt that I did alright.

I felt a little in control with more staff on duty. But this feeling soon disappeared when the telephone rang.

The houseman informed me that there were two more patients to be admitted: one with history of renal colic and one with an acute anal fissure who would need an operation later on. The houseman and I knew that there were not enough empty beds left for the ward. The doctors were aware of this and had already checked and told us that two patients who were on the way to recovery could be transferred to a convalescent ward nearby.

I had to contact relatives and inform the patients and arrange for an ambulance to take them. The patients' properties had to be packed and clean beds had to be made.

Fortunately, the junior sister offered to do most of the tasks involved and did comment to me that it was an indeed extraordinarily busy day. I think that my face showed fatigue and I did somewhat dispirited.

Sister Rigsby said, 'Nurse Poon, it has been so busy. You must have a break and get some lunch.'

So I went to have quick lunch in the canteen.

Mike, the houseman was also in the canteen. He came by and had a cup of coffee with me.

'How is it going, Patrick?'

'Well, it has been so busy. I cannot see how I can pass the assessment.'

'Look, Patrick, it probably is one of the busiest days I

have ever worked here. And you are a good worker.' Mike was being kind and supportive. 'Good luck, anyway.'

I went back to the ward and there was a mountain of paperwork to write. It was the ward routine that once the late shift was on the ward, the nurse in charge on the late shift would take over from the ward. I was in the office to write but everything in the ward seemed to be under control.

Unexpectedly, Sister Rigsby brought a tray of tea into the office. She said, 'Well, Nurse Poon, you have done enough today. Let's have a cup of tea and talk about your assessment.'

I stopped my work and appreciated the refreshment and I said, 'Thanks sister.'

'How do you think you have done, Patrick?' For the first time, she called me Patrick.

'Not very good, Sister. It's been so busy.'

'Have you done any harm to the patients?' She asked.

'Oh, no, they all had proper care. Perhaps we did not have enough time to talk to them.'

'Okay, if I had been in charge, it would have been just the same, because we did not have enough staff.'

'Your judgment of the burst abdomen was good since you had not come across this before. Your handling and care for the patients has been good. They told me you were a good nurse. And you have run the ward well considering that it has been very busy. There were things not done because we had no staff. But overall you have been safe; therefore I have decided to pass you.'

I was so relieved, 'Thanks very much Sister.'

'Well done, Nurse Poon.' Sister Rigsby shook my hand. 'Finish your paperwork and go home.'

I did as I was told. Many nurses, including the second

sister, came in to congratulate me including Mike the houseman. I was very happy.

I stayed on the ward for further six weeks and Sister Rigsby asked me three times to accompany her on the ward rounds with the surgical consultants so that I could learn more. She knew that I wanted to learn and taught me well. In spite of her reputation as a blunt ward sister I had learnt much from her. And I will never forget my very busy day of clinical assessment on her surgical ward.

2 Sister Harris, 1972.

When I was a student nurse I lived in the male nurses' home three miles from the main hospital and the female nurses' home. A group of male student nurses would often talk female nurses and the ward sisters. Sister Harris was probably the most popular of all. She was the senior ward sister of a surgical ward, good looking and in her early thirties. She was friendly and kind to patients and staff.

Fortunately, her ward was on our rotation plan and all the male nurses liked her because she enjoyed the teaching student nurses. She had a good figure and was attractive, just like some pretty nurses you see on television. I recalled that two male students really liked her and they had seen her in a sexy outfit at a party. She was trendy and very well liked by everyone, even the female staff.

Doctors liked her too because she was knowledgeable and easy to get on with. As most doctors were men, they liked the company of a pretty female colleague. But the staff she recruited to work for her on the ward were very nice too, attractive and good nurses. Male nurses like us could not wait to work on her ward.

Sadly, when my turn came, I only worked with her for three weeks on day duty because I had to do the night duty there. Sister Harris told me that I was the only one who could match her for making the beds so quickly and efficiently. When she taught us in the treatment room on some surgical cases, most of us men were lost in admiration of the appearance and demeanour. It was just good to be in the company of a pretty woman.

She probably was aware that she was attractive but she did not flirt with male doctors or male nurses. Some sisters in the hospital were going out with doctors and some became mistresses of certain medical consultants. Sister Harris was happily married with a young son and her husband did not work at the hospital.

She told me once that I was unusual and I asked for the reason. She told me that her staff commented to her that I read poems and not paperbacks on war or thrillers during night duty. At one time there were three or four male students sleeping around with female nurses. I supposed that male nurses did not have good reputation.

Sister Harris was a model of a good ward sister, she was good at everything. She did it well and moreover she did it with charm and grace.

3 Sister Faulkner, 1976.

I was applying for a promotion as a junior charge nurse. In those days getting a job was easier, especially if one was willing to move. I was working in Kettering and the new job was at the Manor Hospital, Walsall, West Midlands.

At that time, I had just passed the Diploma in Nursing part A, a hard and rare qualification. This helped me to get the interview for the post of ward sister. I was applying for the post on a surgical ward, but at the interview the senior staff told me that they had advertised the job wrongly and the post was for a medical ward sister. In view of my qualification they reckoned that I could do the job on the medical ward and I was offered the post. It was promotion, after all, I thought and I accepted the job. So I became a medical charge nurse by default and I moved from Kettering to Walsall. I was to work on an acute medical ward and I had much to learn. I only worked with the senior sister for two weeks before she left. Sister Faulkner was recruited to the medical ward as a senior sister.

She was in her forties, very old fashioned and a distant person. However she must have been experienced to have been recruited to the post.

She was quiet, a kind of person one might not want to ask questions. This was not exactly a good attribute in a nurse, let alone a ward sister. Our ward clerk was a woman who was an inquisitive sort. She found out that Sister Faulkner was a spinster as many ward sisters were then, and that she lived some thirty five miles away.

The ward clerk thought that the new sister was okay and she could humour her. The student nurses, however, found Sister was odd and distant and informed me of this. I tried to support the Sister Faulkner by saying that all people were different and that she was a very experienced nurse.

I had always enjoyed teaching and Sister Faulkner was pleased and allocated me to look after the students on rotation.

Students like the idea because I was young and energetic. I planned the programme of teaching student nurses which included the drugs commonly used on the ward, myocardial infarction, asthma, epileptics and bronchitis.

The junior doctors disliked Sister Faulkner but dared not tell her. They found her unapproachable. The ward sister had a habit of bleeping junior doctors every twenty minutes till the jobs were done after a consultant's ward round. This was irritating for them, especially when the junior doctors were dealing with more important issues on the ward. The junior doctors told me that they knew if I bleeped them they would know it was about something important and they would come to the ward immediately.

The consultants were informed and some of then complained to the nursing officer of the medical unit. The nursing officer asked me for my view. I did not know what to say as I was a colleague. The nursing officer asked me of it was true that some staff said she drove a small car and left her dog in the car all day in the care park. I said that I did not know and I worked mostly opposite her shift.

The nursing officer asked me if Sister Faulkner showed a caring attitude towards the patients. I had never been asked such a question before and I was hesitant with an answer. I answered tactfully I thought that the patients thought she was okay but they knew she was not a warm person. I did not say this but at times, I did wonder why the senior officers employed her.

Altogether I worked with her for two years. I learnt very little from her. She had made herself quite unpopular in the hospital. We did not become friends. After two years of working with her, I applied and got a senior charge nurse post on a surgical ward in the same hospital.

Sister Faulkner did not stay too long and she left soon after. I thought there must have been many nurses like her working in hospital every two or three years and then they moved on.

I had learnt something from working with her. I learnt that I must not be like her, so distant and unapproachable. She might be knowledgeable in medicine but in nursing, one must be more caring and social and warm to the patients and staff.

Tale 15

The concept of pain

'We listen to others to discover that we ourselves believe.'
George Grant.

One of the man reasons that patients were admitted to hospital was the suffering of pain. Usually it was severe pain that warranted hospitalisation, investigations and treatment. The most severe pain was normally treated with a morphine related drug, a form of heroin that caused the patient to hallucinate and relaxed, making the sufferer forget his pain.

In England, morphine related drug belonged to a group of drugs called the controlled drugs. These drugs could be used as a pain relief but it was possible for the patients to become addicted to them. Using it in hospitals or care homes, the drug must be checked by a trained nurse and another person. A strict procedure must be adhered to, such as the ordering, using and the disposal of the drugs.

In the seventies, the controlled drug was used commonly and regularly to control pain. At times, it was used with another strong sedative to alleviate pain. The drug could be only used four hourly as it could kill the patient. In those days, for patients with bad pain, the controlled drug was added to an intravenous infusion to control the pain on a continuous basis. Then, these drugs could be used in a pump to deliver the painkillers more steadily. The pump was attached to a drip stand and pumped in steadily to the patient.

Certainly, it was sad to see many patients in different forms of pain such as rollicking colicky pain, dull but continuous pain, pain that could disturb one's sleep. No wonder soon afterwards, pain clinic was created and specialists were created and different skills were developed.

In the nineties, mobile pumps could be used for patients to control the pain by increasing the dosage of the controlled drug. It was good to see patients more mobile by using a portable pump better than confined to a bed or a chair. Sometimes, patients could alter the speed of the drug used.

In due course, palliative care was developed. Nurses were trained to care for dying patients and the care of pain was the essential part of that care. I have always admired nurses working in this specialty because I could not do it. I could not nurse the dying or the care of children continuously though I was quite happy to care for acutely ill patients suffering from medical or a surgical complaint.

Such was the dynamics and varieties in nursing these days. When I was a deputy of a nursing home, specialising in convalescence, elderly care and palliative care, I came across poor dying patients suffering with sever pain. At St. Mary's Nursing home, where I worked for two years, I nursed some unfortunate dying priests suffering with these agonies of pain. At the home, I witnessed for the first time the old fashioned pastoral care conducted mostly by the nuns there. It was enriching to behold such loving care and it was done for free by good hearted nuns who would talk with and listen to such patients. They had all the time in the world and were so patient with the sick, they were caring. The development of pain therapy by mobile pump was indeed a very good development for patients.

*

Derek was a good tennis player but he has suffered from bad back for many years. The bad back prevented him from playing tennis and he decided to go to see a doctor. On X-rays, he was found to have some unusual curvature in his spine and he was on the waiting list to have an operation. Last year, he had three operations to overcome the pain and he was recovering so well that he could still play some tennis which was the passion in his life.

In one outpatient appointment, he was seen by a different doctor who looked at his x-rays and found that it was beyond his belief that Derek was not on stronger analgesics. Derek replied that his pain was not too bad. The doctor insisted Derek must attend the pain clinic to have good advice and treatment for his pain.

At first, Derek thought that his pain was not so bad and that it was quite manageable and he was not sure that he should even attend the clinic. But when the day came, it was quiet at work so he decided that he would go and keep the appointment. During the session, the specialist nurses could not believe that he could walk around so well without severe pain. So, Derek was prescribed very strong analgesics to deal with the pain. Derek further explained that his pain was not so bad as to warrant such strong painkillers.

But the nurses told him that by taking the tablets, his pain would be better managed. The nurses were not convinced that he was not in pain. Derek was in a dilemma because he did not like taking tablets. However, he decided not to take them. His pain did not increase and he was enjoying his tennis.

Derek could not believe that his clinical findings by doctor and specialists could paint such a different picture to his real living. Perhaps his pain threshold was high and he did not require more painkillers. Why did the professionals believe that their treatment was needed and did not listen to what Derek was saying? How could the views be so different? The concept of pain surely must be dependent on the own individual.

Tale 16

Carol, the care assistant – 1997

'A tale never loses its telling.'
A proverb.

I was newly appointed as a full time staff nurse in a nursing home in Derby. I was next in line after a matron who has been working there for nine months and we seemed to be getting on together well. There were also three part time staff nurses who had been working there much longer.

Unlike working in a hospital where one seemed to have more trained nurses and less care assistants, we were quite alone working in a nursing home. Usually we had one trained staff nurse or at most two on duty and so we had to rely heavily on care assistants. More decisions had to be made by the nurses because there were no doctors about on hand.

In a care home, some people said with sarcasm when talking about care assistants. 'You pay peanuts; you get monkeys. This certainly implied that the quality of some the care assistants were not good.

Janet, the matron, was very aware of the difficulty of getting and keeping staff. They were generally on the minimal wage and indeed some were not very committed. In our nursing home, about half of the day duty carers were good and had been working there for some time. This was a good sign. On night duty, there also seemed to be a stable workforce.

There was always headache when staff was off sick and finding replacement was not easy. Often the management had to plea with staff to do the extra shifts. The owners did not like using agency staff because of the expense. Being a matron in the care home usually had many staffing problems, especially with night duty.

Janet had done her night shift round to get to know the staff. She once told me there were one or two intimidating night carers but they were reliable. In the past, the matron or the owner turned a blind eye to night problems because of the particular difficulty in replacing them. Kate, the night staff nurse, has been on night duty for fifteen years. She was a reliable staff. She would always turn up on duty no matter what the weather was. But she was not a strong character and would let some night carers take advantage of her.

*

On one evening shift, I was on duty in the home with a bank staff nurse. The shift went well and we were relaxing, having a cup of tea. She turned to me and said, 'The carers here are pretty decent and they are well-mannered.'

'Good, why wouldn't they?' I replied.

'Well, Patrick, some fifteen miles from here, there is a nursing home and they found difficulty getting staff. Most of the carers talk loudly and swear a lot.'

'That's terrible.' I said.' We have our code of conduct and demand a certain level of courtesy.'

'Well, it's a town full of miners and a lot of them swear very badly.'

'Oh.'

'But the carers are their wives and they swear too.'

'I would warn them.' I said.

'Someone tried and lost three carers in short order so the owner applied pressure on the staff and asked her to let them be.'

'Really? I'd rather leave.' I said.

'Well, Patrick, many of the staff need the money and cannot leave.' The staff nurse replied.

'Certainly, it is a difficult situation but we all have to abide by the rule.'

*

One morning, Janet did a round with the residents and found Mary, an elderly resident, was tearful and distressed. Janet asked for the reason but Mary seemed reluctant to say. The carers did say that she had been incontinent during the two nights and she was not happy. But Janet sensed that something was wrong.

Half an hour later, Janet returned with two cups of tea and Mary was happier that the new matron had taken time with her.

'It is quite a nice morning, Mary.'

'Yes, matron.'

'You can call me Janet.' Janet placed her hand on Mary's hand, showing some warmth and compassion.

'No, I'd rather not.' Mary was an old fashioned lady but she seemed to be happier.

'Mary, I sense that something is not right and I am sorry that you were wet again last night.'

Mary was quiet.

'Did the carers not do the two hourly toileting with you?'

The resident did not reply. She looked frightened.

'Whatever you say to me, Mary, will remain confidential and I will protect you.'

'Are you sure?' Mary seemed to have obtained some courage from somewhere.

'Yes, that is why I am here.' Janet looked at Mary in the eyes with kindness.

'Did someone not bother to take you to toilet?'

The silence spoke a thousand words.

'But she was so intimidating and some of us are scared of her?'

'Did she say something to you?'

' She said that she did not sleep during the day and wanted no one to disturb her during the night, otherwise there'll be trouble........'

Janet shook her head in dismay.

'So I'd rather wet myself than ask her for help.'

Janet knew all the staff on duty the previous night. There was Carol, the care assistant on night duty and Amy, a meek and laid back care assistant. Kate, the weak staff nurse, was in charge on that night. Janet could envisage that Carol would dominate the night staff and the residents.

'What can you do to help, matron?' asked Mary.

'Do you mind, Mary, if I write it all down and you sign it?

'No, but how about the carers?'

'It's neither Kate nor Amy, is it?' Janet asked.

Mary thought a little and shook her head in agreement. Janet suggested to Mary that she would discuss the matter with the management and ensure that Carol would not be on duty that night. It so happened that Carol was not scheduled to work that night.

*

Janet rang Kate, the meek staff nurse, who was on duty the previous nights. Kate said that as far as she knew, all residents had two hourly toileting unless they were asleep. She did not actually see the carers do it but she was fairly sure that they did. Janet, however, was not sure that the toileting had taken place.

When Amy was asked on the phone, she said that she always followed Carol's instruction because she has been working at the home longer and she acknowledged that Carol was the senior. Amy said that she was tired but she vaguely recalled that whichever residents were awake during the night were toileted. Janet was not totally satisfied with all the answers because the staff she had just talked to was weak characters.

Derek, the owner of the home, was in the office. Janet informed him of the complaint. Derek felt that he was in a dilemma. He knew that Carol could be loud and intimidating but she was very reliable and always turned up for work. Getting night staff was so difficult and if Derek relied on agency staff he would have to pay far more to keep the home running.

On the other hand, Janet was correct to say that this incident was an act of abuse, an emotional abuse, and that the Social Services took it very seriously. In fact, in recent years, there had been documents sent to care homes on the issues. If words get out about this abuse, the Home would get a bad reputation and in future, it might not have many referrals of clients to the home.

Derek was thinking aloud what he should do. Should Derek act on the complaint or get rid of Janet, the matron? How about Patrick, the second-in-line? Do I have to get rid of him as well?

Janet went back to work in the home. After three hours of deliberation, Derek informed Janet that he would see Carol about the complaint. He asked Carol to his office at 16.00 with Janet.

*

At 16.00, Carol came in the Derek's office. She looked quite tired and it looked as if that she just got out of bed. She was a small woman but with a loud voice. She did not look at all pleased to be there.

Derek asked her to sit in the office which she did.

'I am sorry to drag you in here today and thanks for coming.' Derek said.

'Well, it'd better be good as I could have done with more sleep. Good job I am not working to night.'

'You know Janet, the matron.' Derek continued the conversation.

'Yes.' Carol replied in a low voice.

'Well, I am sorry to say there has been an allegation by one of the residents.' Janet started.

'Who?' Carol asked instantly.

'I do not want to reveal the name yet.'

'Right, what did she say?'

'She said that she was apprehensive of asking you to toilet her during the night and as a result, she became rather wet.'

'How ridiculous, these old people, half of them cannot

remember what they have eaten. And she was accusing me of this.' Carol was not pleased and certainly looked rather intimidating. One could see why the residents would be fearful and tried to avoid her.

'Well, she seems to be quite lucid.' Janet said.

'Well, do you believe her?'

'Yes.'

'Are there any witnesses?'

'Not sure. But there's no smoke without fire.'

'Janet, I know who complained but there does not seem to have any witnesses.' Carol had obviously rung her night colleagues before she came to the interview.

Derek was observing Carol's behaviour and was thinking what to do next. He could not have such an abusive member of staff working in his home; even if it cost him more to find a replacement. Janet was looking at Derek for a decision.

'You know what, Carol.' Janet perused the conversation,' I would like you to know that I am starting an investigation while you are having nights off.'

Carol shrugged her shoulder.

'You know I have been working here for ten years and I know when I first met you, you did not like me and now you want to get rid of me.'

'That's not true. I treat everyone fairly and this is a serious allegation, an abuse, in fact.'

'What?' Carol was intrigued.

'It is called an emotional abuse.'

'You know, half of the staff here are quite quiet and I happen to talk more and I get penalised because of it.'

'Well, have you been toileting the residents during the nights?'

'Yes, but sometimes they are asleep and we do not wake them up.'

'Well, I do not want residents to be too frightened to call for help and they get wet though.'

'Well, they could have pressed the call button.' Carol said.

Derek intervened, 'Okay, Carol, we are investigating and will write to you and let you know. I know that you have been a reliable member of the night staff but we have to find out.'

'Have you been on any courses on abuse, Carol?' Janet asked.

'No, I know all about it.' Her face implied that she did not want to know and she looked annoyed. 'You know after all my years of service here, this is what I get, hassles!'

'So, am I working next week here?' Carol asked. She knew the insecurity of care home work.

'We shall write to you.' Derek said.

Carol was becoming more and more angry, 'If I leave and resign, I shall take you to industrial tribunal for compensation!!' Carol stormed off the office.

*

Janet and Derek looked at each other. Both felt that they had made the right decision.

'Can you cover without her?' Derek asked.

'I shall try. I certainly do not want an intimidating person working here. This will give us a bad name.'

'But I do not want to use any agency staff, ok?'

'OK, I shall see if I can find any more facts from the night staff about the incident.'

*

The questioning gathered no more solid information about Carol's behaviour. Janet and Derek were disappointed. It was said that Carol's husband was not a pleasant character. I was advised by Janet that we should park our cars near our office so that the vehicles might not be damaged by intruders. An air of unease was around us. If there was no solid allegation against the care assistant, we could not proceed with disciplinary procedure.

But it could not be easy for Carol to continue working for the home, we thought, because people seemed to know about her character. The care home was a small place and everyone knew what was happening. Legally, Carol could resign and to take the home to industrial tribunal for constructive dismissal. This could cost the home thousands of pounds.

It was no surprise to note Carol rang in sick the following week and Janet had to find cover. Fortunately, Janet managed by asking other members of staff to work overtime. Because of the length of Carol's service, she was entitled to have sick pay. This was the first time that Carol had been challenged about her behaviour. Over the years, staff and residents had just put up with her. Her position was solid because it was very difficult to find night duty cover.

Three weeks went by and Carol remained off sick due to stress and she was still entitled to sick pay. Derek wrote to her, inviting her to an interview with Janet and Derek. But she did not reply. We were pondering what she would do. We heard the rumour from other night staff that she was going to resign and to take us to industrial tribunal.

Six weeks later, she did put in her resignation and saying that she would take the Home to industrial tribunal because of constructive dismissal. It was a relief to all staff that she was not coming back.

Derek and Janet consulted the Home's solicitor and were told that it would be a difficult case to defend because it was the case of the resident's complaint versus Carol's statement. But would Carol go through with the ordeal of an industrial tribunal?

Janet and I continued to work in the nursing home with a feeling of unease, cautious of the safety of our cars, in case the car tyres might be slashed. We knew the Tribunal would be an unpleasant case and we were unlikely to win. We heard that Carol already had found work and was working somewhere in a factory.

In due course, the night care became much better. Regular toileting was done and Mary was happier. She was dry and was thankful for what Janet has done for her.

Months went on and it was clear that Carol's intention was only an empty threat. She never did take us to an industrial tribunal. The industrial tribunal would not have done any good to her and her name either. But it was her intimidating behaviour that was damaging to everyone. The Nursing Home recruited a better care assistant in due course for the night duty.

Nursing homes looked after many residents who were mostly vulnerable. A few intimidating staff could make life miserable for both residents and staff. Most staff members were too nice and did not want trouble and would not challenge bad behaviour of some staff members. It took courage and integrity to challenge such situation. Janet was one of the most courageous trained nurses that I have seen and have had the pleasure to work with.

Tale 17

Jack, the carer

'I feel a feeling which I feel you all feel'

-a sermon

'So, Patrick, you are a male nurse?'

'Yes, I am.'

'Were you happy being a male nurse then?'

'Yes, it has given me a fairly good life, I cannot complain.'

'You know, in the 50s, nearly all male nurses were homosexuals.'

'Really, I heard that. I was not in UK then. Things have changed. I have a family with a wife, children and a granddaughter.'

'Good for you. But being a male in a female environment is not easy?'

'You are right. You sound like you have had some experience with this.'

'Well, my mother has. Shall I tell you about Jack, her carer?'

'Ok, I have the time.'

'My mother is 82 years old, living on her own and the social services supply her with a carer. Female carers, she is ok with that. Then, one day, the social service rang to say they are short of staff, asking if they can allocate a male carer to her.'

'Oh, how did she take it?' I asked.

'Not well, she refused. She thought that it was inappropriate a male looking after a woman.'

'Some women patients like it.'

'I know, some do. The social service rang to say they have tried, either she is to do without a carer or have a male cover.'

'Oh, she would not like that.'

'No, she does not. But I said to my mum that male doctors see her and examine her. What is the difference? Luckily, she relented.'

'Well done, did she like Jack? What is he like?'

'He is nice, a good and kind carer and polite with her. He is tall but nice. Mum is ok with him. Three weeks went by, she prefers him to the female carers. He makes jokes and she likes it.'

'I have the same experiences. In two nursing homes, when some women residents knew I was on duty, they asked for me, so the female carers said. Males give them some sort of excitement.'

'And sometimes, women can be bitchy.'

I nodded in agreement.

'Two months have gone by and they now get on very well. However female carers still attend to her at times.'

'Okay.'

'But sometimes, female patients or residents take advantage of male carers or male nurses too, don't they?'

'I know.' I said.

'How?'

'You really want to know?'

'Yes.'

'Mm, at times, some female residents knew female nurses

will be on duty and they play up, they ask me to do a PR on them?'

'What is a PR?'

'Per rectum examination means sticking a finger up the bottom to feel if she is impacted.'

'Oh, what did you do?'

'I would not do it; they could wait for the female nurses on duty to do them. And they have been like that for a while.'

'Oh, I get it. You mean, the female would prefer a sexual feel if a man does it?'

'Exactly. Other male nurses have experienced this request before.'

'Crafty devils. That is some women!'

'So your mum is happy with Jack then?'

'Well, the story has not finished yet. She fell and broke her hip and she was in hospital for ten weeks.'

'That is the finish of their relationship then?'

'Oh, no. No carer visited my mum except Jack.'

'Good on him.'

'She was so thankful and Jack really cares for her. Sometimes, he shops for her as a friend.'

'Nice to hear that. There are many good male carers.'

'On her discharge home, my mum asks for no one else to care for her but Jack.'

I was pleased to hear the progress.

'Eventually, she had to go to a care home. And she had to sell her house. Jack bought her house and they are very good friends still.'

17A

The Mountain

I think that I am quite certain that there's nothing as majestic as the mountain.
They stand there high and mighty,
through passion, love, misery and eternity.

The Colorado Rocky Mountain stands so high, through the rain, cold, wind and the sunshine.
I admire the snow-capped Blackcomb at Whistler,
with the skiers down the slope fast.

And how about the beautiful mountains at Switzerland,
So quiet and serene as if you were in the dreamland.

In Hong Kong, the mighty Lion Rock stares,
guarding its people and their stocks and shares.

It is said the Lords of the Mountains guard,
its people, its land and its heart.

So go tell it to the Mountain,
your wishes, blessings and things uncertain.

I am glad the range of the mountains reign,
so that I can cry, laugh and I sing.

Patrick K S Poon

June, 2013

Year 2000s

Tale 18

Car accident in Cyprus ...1990s

'I can always rely on the kindness of strangers.'
Tennessee Williams

In the last many years, statistically, road traffic accidents have always been one of the top five killers in the United Kingdom. I do not know that statistics in different parts of the world. But it seems that there are more and more cars on the road and not many new roads have been built to help ease the traffic.

My wife and I enjoy our holidays abroad, for the warm weather and to be away from it all. It was our first time we went to Cyprus, a hot country. The location was by the sea with lovely sea breeze blowing coolly by.

One evening, we went to have dinner some thirty minutes away from our hotel. At about 10.15 pm., we left the restaurant. I was driving and my wife, Jane, was sitting by my side and Andy, our son, was sitting at the back. I was not a fast driver and was enjoying the moonlight and the sea breeze. I was driving on a main road. It was not busy but suddenly, I saw a car just moving across the road. It was so sudden that I braked sharply but I was too late. The car wheels squeaked and I could feel the tyres braking very sharply. My car hit the other car with quite a force and it turned round 360 degrees. The car was smashed up and I could feel myself in a zone of surreal situation.

I became unusually quiet and got out of the car. It was the worst car crash caused by driving ever. People were gathering around. I asked if my wife was okay. She said that she would need her neck checked. My youngest son, Andy, was sitting at the back and luckily, he was sitting with his seatbelt on and he was unhurt.

All the cars behind me stopped. A young man came out to reassure me that the driver should not have made a three point turn in the middle of the busy road.

On examining that car, the driver seemed to be hurt on his chest, his wife seemed unhurt and a baby by her seemed to be okay too. At the back of the car, there was a crate of beer with half of it empty. The driver did smell strongly of alcohol. I was relieved to note the young man was volunteering to say the other driver was in the wrong. I replied that I was not a fast driver and it was fortunate that I was not and tried the brake very sharply. One could see the tyres marks of my car on the road.

Before long, the police car came and the kind man who happened to be a Cypriot was talking to the Police in their native tongue. By their facial expression, the Police seemed to know the other driver was in the wrong and the young man was to be the witness. Amongst the crowds of people watching, there were a couple who happened to have been in the same restaurant with us. He recognised us and said that we were staying in the same hotel. I was happy to know this and I asked if they minded if he stayed with us, since we would not have the transport to get back to the hotel. They were nice and agreed.

The ambulance came and took my wife to have a neck checked out and fortunately, she was okay. The wife and the baby from the other car were okay but the other driver had sustained three broken ribs. The whole process took more than an hour and the kindness of the Cypriot and the couple from the hotel was much appreciated by my wife and me. We made a statement and the Police mainly took it from the Cypriot.

Three hours later, the couple took us back to the hotel. The experience was surreal and the journey on the ambulance was quite unsafe, by English standards. I thanked the couple and the Cypriot very sincerely.

The following day, I rang the car hire company and it seemed that car accidents were quite common. The Cypriot driving was not up to the British standard. The kind Cypriot came to our hotel with the police and asked us further questions. Again, I thanked the young man and offered to pay for his time and kindness but he refused.

I enquired if the family was okay and was told that we were all fortunate that we were. The driver with the broken ribs would stay in the hospital for a few more days and would be charged with the dangerous driving.

We continued our holiday and in quite a low key way. But thankfully, since the accident, we had no other accidents with cars. On reflection, we were indeed very lucky. It could have been much worse. Who said that there were no kind people in the world? With this experience, I truly believe that there is much kindness from strangers.

Tale 19

Nurses' fear

'None but a coward dares to boast that he has never known fear.'
Fardinard Foch.

When I was first recruited in nursing in 1968, my specialty was in mental nursing. There were comments from some people that it was unusual for a man to be a nurse, I paid no attention to that and it did not deter me. In Hong Kong, psychiatric nursing meant crazy people and violence and fear because many people thought that mental patients could harm people. Some people would not want to work in that environment but I was not in awe of it.

On my first day of training, we were advised that there were indeed many violent and psychotic patients in the hospital. When we stood to observe them, we were advised that we must stand in front of a wall or wire fence so that no one could attack us from behind and hitting by patients on staff members was not uncommon. Patients were kept on locked ward. On duty, we were given a key which could open all the locked doors in the mental hospital. We had to take good care of the key; we had to sign in and out when dealing with the ward key.

On two chronic wards, there were few patients called

Mongols (Down's syndrome). In these days, they would be called patients suffering from learning disabilities. They were the unfortunate children of some patients suffering from GPI (general paralysis of insane-an illness caused by syphilis and the bacteria attacked the back of the eyes so that those patients walked with a particular gait). Their blood was infectious and they could infect us via the blood stream. Therefore, we were warned about the need to wash our hands after injections. In those days, we did not have the facilities of wearing gloves or using disposable gloves. Syringes and needles were sterilised on the wards.

Needless to say, nurses had the fear of being infected and we indeed washed hands vigorously after giving injections. Fortunately, we had not heard of any illness passed on from patients there. From the medical side, some doctors informed us that some poor housemen got infected with tuberculosis and later died.

When I started training in England in the 1970s, nurses were advised to lift properly, especially on geriatric wards (called elderly care wards nowadays). We all had various form of training and forms of lifting techniques so that we could lift properly such as the 'Australian lift'. Hoists were not used at that time.

Personally I did have a little spell of bad back when working on geriatric wards but thankfully, I was in good health and quickly recovered. However, complaints of bad back in nurses were common because many patients were heavy to life. Indeed, some members of staffs sued the hospital or health authorities successfully and the NHS had to pay out thousands of pounds in compensation. It was not uncommon in those days to hear of a nurse quitted nursing because of a bad back.

Many years later, hoists were introduced and the staff had to use them to avoid bad problems. Risk assessment forms were introduced and used to assess what equipment to use to avoid the occurrence of a bad back.

When I was a charge nurse of the medical and surgical wards in Walsall, I was very aware of the area being one of the most deprived areas in the country. We had many admissions of tuberculosis, scabies and other infectious diseases. I was very aware of the nursing procedure of washing hands and wearing gowns and adhering to barrier nursing procedure. After admitting scabies patients, I tended to scratch more and I was sure that it was due to psychological reason. However, we did have regular Xray checkups. I remember well that in one of my x-rays, I was told that I had a scar that might have been an immune tuberculosis scar caught from one of my patients. Fortunately, I was told that I should be okay in the future.

One of our roles was teaching student nurses and it was my duty to show some dressing techniques to some students, at least, three students fainted. I was not sure that it was their fears to the dressing procedures or the sight of the surgical wounds. It could have been the first time they saw a new wound. Fortunately, they survived the ordeal and they carried on with their nursing careers.

In the 1980s, nurses and doctors had to mix the cytotoxic drugs for patients suffering from cancer. Big needles were used to mix fluids with the drug and I used to help doctors to prepare the drug which was a lengthy procedure.

Many years later, I learnt that preparing those cytotoxic drugs was now a very sterile procedure. It was done in the pharmacy and the staffs had to wear goggles, gloves and gowns, under the strict sterile procedure. In the old days, we were never told to use gloves, gowns and goggles. I distinctly remember that I even had some drugs spilled on my skin during the procedure when I was mixing it with a doctor.

Talking with my contemporaries, I was reminded that in our younger days in 1970s we were often left in charge of the wards. When we were not sure of what to do, we informed our senior nurses and often, we were told that they were too busy and we had to do what we thought was right. We were troubled by this but the responsibilities lay with the senior nurses.

According the British Medical Association, there were certain common illnesses found amongst doctors. These illnesses were often associated with the stress of the job. Alcoholism, overdoses and drug abuse were to be quite common. Even suicides occurred.

Aggression from patients was what we nurses feared the most. It could be from psychiatric patients, drunks or patients who had taken an overdose. I used to dread working at the weekends nursing patients who had overindulged in drinks or drugs. In the morning, many of them vomited or urinated in bed. They were not 'with it' at all and could not be reason with. I did not blame female nurses not wanting to go near them and often help would be sought from the porters.

In my nursing career, I have known one female nurse who was hit and went off sick; also a male nurse who was hit in the eye, and thus warranted an operation. He was off sick for months.

Stress was common amongst nurses. This was due to the continuous facing of patients' illnesses and keeping with deadlines to medical and nursing procedures. There were many stressed nurses that I knew who received treatment of counselling. They were off sick for a long period.

Did we nurses fear for ourselves because we did not sleep well and were worried about different things on the wards? I remember it well that twice I woke up in the middle of the night and rang the hospital staff to relay information that I had forgotten at the handovers.

After continuous working, sometimes, nurses seemed to take many days to relax and then to start to enjoy their holidays. Subconsciously nurses had to be very careful to think what they have encountered, so that they would not to catch any infectious diseases. The caution and fear are always there.

Tale 20

Mrs Hever, Senior Nursing Officer

'A friend in need is a friend indeed.'

When I was a charge nurse on a medical ward in 1976, Mrs. Hever was a senior nursing officer of the Walsall hospitals. She was a thin and tall lady and a nurse. She was old fashioned but caring and strict. Some staff was apprehensive of her because of her appearance. She must have been in her forties or fifties.

For some reason we always got on well though she was not my direct boss. Her husband worked on night duty as a bank staff nurse on our ward and we got on well.

Then I became a senior charge nurse on the surgical ward. The only dealings I had with Mrs. Hever were when she was on call. She would ring my ward to find out if I had empty beds. I worked on the surgical ward for more than two years, learning and enjoying myself. Then the post holder, a surgical nursing officer, was going to retire.

In my yearly appraisal, I always expressed that I would like to get on in my career. In the world of nursing, there were broadly only two routes, to teach at the college of nursing or management. Although I enjoyed teaching student nurses and newly qualified nurses, I was not sure which way I would go.

The senior hospital staff, including Mrs. Hever asked me

if I would like to serve as an acting nursing officer, surgery before it was advertised. I accepted and did the job for three months. The transition was not easy because most of the ward sisters were older and more experienced than me. I was thirty-one years old and felt they were more experienced nurses than me.

Another difference was that I was no longer the leader of a specific ward but of four surgical wards, including an ear, nose and throat ward and a gynaecological ward which I was not expert in. Mrs. Hever reassured me that management was management and it did not matter what specialities one had experience of.

She was correct. Many years on, in the NHS hospitals, there were senior managers such as chief executives with years of experiences in other industries recruited to run hospitals. Still, I was in a state of quiet turmoil regarding the position. But I did apply for the post of nursing officer of the surgical wards at Manor hospital and got the job. Mrs. Hever congratulated me and I thanked her for all her support.

As a nursing officer, I found it very difficult to come to terms with the fact there were not enough staff on the wards mainly because of sickness. There was no extra money to recruit more staff. Mrs Hever pointed out that we had to run the hospitals within the budget. She was right and I felt that perhaps I was not mentally strong enough.

I helped on the ward by doing drug rounds or dressings if the wards were short of staff. The ward staff appreciated the help. I was trying to change the stigma of a nursing officer

Then the wind of changes was in the air. There were more changes of bosses and they were all seemed very young and were too eloquent. These senior staff did not stay in post for any length of time. After two or three years, they moved on. Reorganisations were there every two to three years. Everyone was feeling uncertain about their jobs.

I realised that computerisation was coming in (year 1982) and I managed to be seconded to do a data processing management course in the local college. It was a good move and I learnt a great deal about computers.

Through another reorganisation, I did not get a post that I wanted and was placed in a post as a charge nurse and nursing officer of surgical wards, an impossible position. Though my salary was protected, I was not happy with the situation. That was the lowest ebb of my nursing career. Fortunately, Mrs. Hever was aware of my situation and offered to have me as her assistant at Walsall General Hospital.

I accepted the job instantly. Mrs. Hever was my saviour at the times of my need. I assisted her on her surgical wards and did a similar job as a nursing officer. She was kind and helpful to me. She gave me breathing space to find my feet to think what I was going to do next. Within three or four months, I applied and got a more senior post as an assistant director of nursing services.

During my years of working at Burton-upon-Trent, Mrs Hever and I kept in touch. The college of nursing at Burton was also in association with Walsall and hence it gave us a chance to meet up.

When I left the NHS to teach at Stephenson College as a lecturer for health and social care from year 2000, I remember a letter she wrote to me, saying she was so proud that I became a lecturer. We met up for lunch once in Lichfield, at which time she was retired. We reminisced about the old times at Walsall and both of us agreed the best times in nursing were as a ward sister, where one could control our domain and ensure that we provided the best care for the patients. She told me that during her last years in Walsall, the younger senior officers were not nice and when the structure of grading came in 1988, she was not graded high. She was treated badly at the end of her long nursing career.

A few years later, her husband rang me to say that Mrs Hever was very ill with cancer and was in Burton hospital. I went to visit her in the side ward. She was ill and I was not sure that she recognised me but I was glad to have visited her and saw her for the last time.

Mrs Hever knew me from 1975 to the 2000s and she was always a great help and support to me. She was my friend. One funny thing was the addressagraph she once gave me as a Xmas present many years ago when she was a senior nursing officer and I was her nursing officer, I still kept it and used often.

20A

A man or butterfly

'I do not know whether I was than a man,
dreaming I was a butterfly or whether I am now a butterfly.'
Huang Tse.

In meditation, I am a butterfly, winging so swiftly across the sky.
And then I'm awoke, I am just a man, wandering so aimlessly across this land.

A man or butterfly, a man or butterfly, flying across the sky;
why, why and why?

Cold wind blows, clouds roll and roll, it's real or unreal, nobody knows.
Such is life. A brink in you eyes. Here, there and everywhere, that's your life.

A man or butterfly, a man or butterfly, flying across the sky;
why, why and why?

Patrick K S Poon
1997.

The generic tales

Tale 21

The Sally Pepper Show – BBC Radio Derby – May, 2013 my view on the NHS changes

'Pleasure is seldom found when it is sought; our brightest blazes of gladness are commonly kindled by unexpected sparks.'

Samuel Johnson

When my first book, 'Tales from a Male Nurse' came out on 25.3.2013, I was attempting to market my book. Many books were sold by word of mouth to some kind and supportive relatives and friends via my website www.pkspoon.co.uk. I thought of contacting the Burton Mail at Burton-upon-Trent where I worked for some eight years in the Burton Hospitals. Some people knew me though I left the town four years ago.

At time, my books could be bought at my local post office at St. Dominick and Waterstones, Burton and my website.

I rang the Burton Mail and a kind and helpful reporter called Adrian was keen to report me. The article came out in April and the impact was more effective than I thought. My books were selling quite well at Burton Waterstones and my daughter rang me up excitedly, 'Dad, your book is at 12th on the best local selling list.' I was speechless and got her to text me the photo. It was an ego trip for me and I was excited.

It was strange to feel that someone I might know or not know has bought my books at the bookshop. Certainly from my website, I have sold some books to strangers. I suppose that I have to get used to it.

The newspaper must have been read by the BBC producer Veena at Derby Radio and she contacted me via email, inviting me for a radio interview at Derby. I was very pleased and sent her a copy of my book to read.

Before the show on the 23.5.2013, a lady rang me at home to find out some background information. She was nice and inquisitive and I was too glad to supply her with the information especially that I was proud to be at the number 12th on the local best seller's list.

The BBC Radio Derby station has been in operation for more than thirty years. It was modern looking and the staffs were very friendly. The receptionist lady was nice and chatty. She made me a cup of tea to try to relax me. I had been interviewed on radio by BBC Truro before and it took about seven minutes. Before long I met with Veena, the producer, who took me into the studio. Derby Radio station was a bigger location with lots of history on the walls. Pictures of well known local presenters were on the walls and it was all done very tastefully.

I was introduced to Sally Pepper of the show. She was an attractive lady with a good manner that made me feel at ease in an instant. I felt that she quite liked me already and certainly she made me feel welcome. I gave her a copy of my book which later she asked me to sign for her. To start with, she informed that today was the first day of an inquiry into Burton Hospital where I once worked. I was not aware of this situation.

I knew that Burton hospital was on the top ten in a list as one of the highest mortality rate in the country. Not good news! She would like to ask for my view on this topic as I once worked there. She would talk to me at the interview about my book in the first half and then we should have some music and then she would ask me for my opinion on the hospital.

I was feeling slightly nervous and was thinking on my feet. I was expecting a seven minutes interview, an in and out job, and never thought that I would be interviewed for so long. I was pleasantly pleased about the promotion of my book but somehow, I felt a bit nervous or cautious about what I ought to say. But I was thinking aloud and ready with the answers.

I answered the questions about my book well (as my friends and relatives told me later) and Sally and discussed some tales in my book. It was spontaneous and enjoyable. In fact, on reflection, it was a pleasure to have been interviewed about my book as well as my view on the Burton Hospital's current poor situation. However, we did not have much time to discuss all the reasons for the decline of some NHS hospitals. Hence, I thought I would explore the topics more fully in print.

NHS and Community Care Act, 1990----Margaret Thatcher's legacy might have done many good things for the UK. but to my mind from the 1990's, she started destroying the NHS. She initiated the internal market to trade the services and hence, there was an army of business managers created in hospitals and hospitals became trusts with directors of estates, finances and non-clinical services. All these senior managers' wages were to be found from the existing budget. Most of them were better paid than the nurses on the wards and mo wonder since then; there have been staff shortage of staffs on the wards which of course affected the quality of services.

Before 1990s, we tried to achieve high standard of care but after 1990, we tried to sustain the good quality of care. All costs of services were looked at and the senior managers decided what services could be run with profit.

Decentralisation of services—from the hospital points of view, it looked at how to get the lowest cost with certain level of services. Before, the ward managers could ring the domestic services in the hospital to complain about the cleanliness on the wards. Now, the ward managers could not because they were not in control of the cleaners. They were accountable to some faceless managers of some company miles away who did not know that much about cleanliness on the ward. It was no wonder there was an increase of bacteria infections. These situations could be read about in the newspapers.

Last week, in a surgery, there was a poster from the BMA (British Medical Association), indicating that they would not like to negotiate services from GPs to other contractor services because the services were only interested in profits not the quality of services to the patients.

At Burton Hospitals, there have been at least four chief executives been and gone since 1997, the year I left. One could imagine what a ward sister thought of this, people coming in making changes and then moving on.

From my friends who still worked in Burton hospital, I had the feeling that some staff were working in the state of uncertainty and mistrust. What a place to work if true! Of one thing I was certain—morale was extremely low and few members of the staff seemed happy at work. They stayed on because it was a job with fairly good income.

By coincidence, in the Independent Newspaper on 17.7.2013, there was an article written on the hospitals with the high mortality rate, including Burton hospital. It stated the same like I have just mentioned. The reasons for the high mortality were staffing, lack of resources that led to infrequent checking of important equipment daily at clinical services. It stated that the real reasons were not because of the clinical staffs but it was due to the incompetence of very senior managers, including the Secretary of the State.

On reflection, most of all these above reasons for the failure of the NHS have been reported in some different forms.

The Sally Pepper Show highlighted that more. In the UK, no one with the real power has the courage to stand up and say all these systems did not work and it needed great changes. The sad reality was many other important services were running in the same fashion.

A friend of mine who has just retired from the Police Department said the similar topic to me, just like what I heard before many years ago, that the Police department was to run like a business (just like the NHS!). Mind boggled that the Police were now looking at fighting crimes with more income than expenditure in mind (a concept of business). No wonder that they were more interested in taking photos from camera on cars speeding than catching murderers because it was more expenditures than income. I wonder if this was true.

However, it was refreshing to know the media like BBC Radio Derby was interested in the views of NHS hospital services and the view of the public like me. Thank you, Sally Pepper and the team.

Tale 22

Janet, the volunteer

'To change and to change for the better
are two different things ...'
A proverb

Janet was a midwife recruited to Saltash, Cornwall, to work as a community midwife in 1995. The main reason for her employment was her vast experience of home birth which she gained in Derbyshire.

The Cornish are a proud people and they wanted their children to be born at home, so they were born Cornish. If not at home, the babies would be born at the nearest hospital, Derriford which was in Devon. Hence, at one time, Saltash had one of the highest home births in the country.

The process of home birth is not a straightforward business. Most times, a home birth would take hours and would require the attention of the midwife who was dedicated to the closeness and joy of home birth. When the woman was actually giving birth, two midwives were required. Janet and the home birth team loved the other aspects of the job such as giving advice over the phone and visiting worried mothers.

From the employers' point of view it was both time-consuming and costly.With cutbacks in funding, homebirths were not allowed to carry on because the NHS simply could not afford it. The mums had to go to a centre to give birth and the NHS could centralise the care and use fewer midwives as a result. Midwives were re-deployed and had other tasks.

In due course, Janet retired from the NHS. With her skills not used, she devoted her time in yoga, tennis and walking along the lovely Cornish coasts. She could not be used as a bank midwife because of home situations. Three years went by and she felt that she had lots to offer and eventually became a volunteer at a breastfeeding centre, funded by the Cornish Council.

With her being an ex-midwife she had credibility and the mothers welcomed her advice. The volunteers were all mothers and they were helpful to the users. Good network was set up and the centre had become one of the best locations offering such good services to the mothers in need, in the country.

One day, Janet received a phone call on her mobile from a very distraught young mother who was having problems with breast feeding. The poor mother was young and had had a Caesarean birth. She was kept only one day in the hospital and was discharged because of shortage of beds. Normally, for such birth, the mother would be kept in longer and would have been advised on breastfeeding.

Janet was told that the NHS midwives were so busy and if she could go to help. The poor young mother was panicky and much stressed.

Janet had the time and talked kindly to the mother on the phone. Her advice was well taken and very soon, the young mother was less panicky and felt relieved, knowing that some one had time for her. All her questions were answered well and she felt so happy and thankful. Janet rang three or four hours later and even offered a home visit. The mother was very grateful.

Four hours later, Janet rang the mother and she was still worried. So Janet went to visit her at home. Her husband was there too and all the queries were answered well. The new parents were happy and were so impressed that a volunteer had helped so willingly and that the service was free. Janet was happy and felt rewarded that she could make such a difference to a person in need.

There are hundreds of volunteers like Janet doing similar good work for the needy. Ironically Janet was now fulfilling a voluntary role which was the same work as she did when she was a paid midwife with the NHS.

Tale 23

My Mother

'God cannot be everywhere, so he made mothers.'

From the 1960s, a census has been taken yearly to gather information about the people living on the island of Hong Kong. That was the first time proper information was gathered about Chinese families. However, because of many Chinese have moved from the Mainland China to Hong Kong it is often very difficult to work on a family tree.

My mother was born in Kwanchow, China in 1910 to a rich family. I have not met her father who was a successful businessman. In those days, like many businessmen who had money, they had wives and mistresses. My Grandmother was his second mistress. My Mum told my sister that he had a generous streak in him that very often he held good dinners for many friends.

She was sent to school in Hong Kong called 'The Sacred Heart School' which was well-known even in my school days in Hong Kong. She was quite a progressive girl and even had the English first name Rose. In my younger days, English names were not given by our parents but by ourselves. If we liked a name, we called ourselves by that name. I was an admirer of an American singer Pat Boone and hence I named myself Patrick. Little did I know that it was an Irish name! Strangely, many years later, I gained an Irish son-in-law and often joked that it was my first connection to the Irish.

In those days in China, males always took priority over females. Girls like my mother were married off by blind date young so that fathers did not have to have the burdens of looking after them. Mother married a man in the hair dressing business and soon they had three children. My father seemingly liked my mother and always was around.

Medicine was very scarce in those days. Cholera swept through Hong Kong and Mother's husband and the first son caught it and died from the disease.

Before her husband died, he was saying to my father that he knew he liked my mother and if he would look after her for him. My father, being a righteous man who loved my Mum, married her though she had two children, despite of strong opposition from his family. In those days, marrying a widow with children was not a common event; especially my mother was some nine years older. I think that my father must have loved my mother very much and I admire his courage in going against his family's wishes.

Four of us were born from Mother by our Father. It was very difficult for Father to raise so many of us as he was working for the Urban Service Department. Needless to say we were not rich. My Mother's mother came to Hong Kong to help out and she never left us. I remember that Mother told us she used to have a friend working for a slaughterhouse and she usually gave her food of intestines, liver and kidneys of pigs or cows to help us. Fortunately, our Grandmother and Mother were very patient and good cooks and we enjoyed the food made by them, no matter what it was. They also sometimes did sowing and odd jobs at home to augment their income.

My brother could remember that Mum had to pawn things at the end of the month simply to have more money for food. I was quite good at English when I was young and I gave private tuition to two Chinese children to earn some a little pocket money. At the end of some months, Mum had to resort to borrowing some money from my piggy bank. However, she always gave it back to me.

When I went to England to start training as a nurse in 1969 I used to send twelve pounds a month to Mother so she could go to the tea house to enjoy some dim-sum. She used to thank me and I enjoyed doing this. I did this monthly for twenty years. It made me feel good that I could help out when I could.

When Hong Kong was occupied by the Japanese the Chinese were treated very badly. Many Chinese men died during the conflict and hence, it was common for married women to remarry again after the war. Most of my aunts have been married more than once.

My Mother was a laid back and soft spoken lady, with a good heart. She always taught us to be good to people so they would in turn be good to you. I never saw her lose her temper or raise her voice to us. At times, because of the soft side of her character, people would take advantage of her but she had a steely side with which to fight back. Once, she had some sort of minor stroke and was told she might not walk again, yet, with sheer determination, she tried and tried and very soon, she was walking normally.

When I was younger and living in England, I often grumble. Once, she wrote me a rare Chinese letter with a saying, 'You live in happiness and you are not aware of it.' These were sound words of wisdom from her and I still possess this rare letter written by her to me.

My mother's laid back attitude suited my Father well because he was hot tempered and had a lot to say. Unfortunately he drank rice wine many times a day and smoked incessantly for many years. But he was the boss of the family.

It was no surprise to me when he had a stroke at his early fifties and became bedridden or wheelchair bound for eleven years. Poor Mum had to look after him for all those years but with good support from my two elder brothers and younger sisters. My Mother fed him, washed him and worked very hard. So then she became the boss and decided things around the house.

During that time, I went home to visit them every two to three years. My two elder brothers gave the real help but I gave them moral and financial support. My Mum told me that my father was thankful for the way she looked after him for those years and he wanted to shake her hands before he died. He did and died at the age of sixty-one. However, Mum was the best nurse in the world because during all years, my father never had a pressure sore and he was well fed and cared for.

Fortunately, my Mother lived another twenty years and had a relatively happier time in the later years. She received a good pension from my father's pension scheme. As her children had jobs and they gave financial support and so she had better standard of living than she ever had before. She travelled to see her relatives in America and Canada and she even came to visit me with my sister and her granddaughter.

I was fortunate enough to be able to visit Hong Kong every three years. Local residents recognised me when My Mother and I went to the teahouse for dim-sum in the early mornings.

In the days of no mobile phones, my mother and I used to

talk every month. If she missed me for any reason, my brother George would ring me up and we chatted. She always said that she missed me and I said that I missed her too.

My Mother always dyed her hair black but for some reason, in the last four years of her life, she decided not to. Her hair was pure white and long and she looked old but gracious.

In October, 2003, my brother George rang me from Hong Kong to say that Mother was very ill and had been admitted to the hospital with a minor stroke. Before then, Mother was seldom ill. She did not have diabetes or hypertension but like most old people, her memory was not good. My college was good and granted me compassionate leave.

I flew from Heathrow airport to Hong Kong.

On the plane, I thought to myself that I have been living in the UK for almost forty years. Time and tide wait for no man. We were all older, and perhaps a little wiser. I arrived in the evening and said hello to Mum. She was a little disorientated because she had just arrived home from hospital, after six days stay. She looked at me blankly. We let her go to sleep and rest again.

The following morning, I went to her bed and gave her a cuddle. She opened her eyes,

'Are you back, Sum(my Chinese name)?'

'Yes, Mum. How are you?'

She shrugged her shoulder, 'My leg hurt. Next time when you come, I shan't be here, you know?'

'Mum, don't say that?' I pecked a kiss on her face. She closed her eyes.

'I am old now….' I was feeling so sad.

Mum was trying to sit up. 'Shall I sit you up, Mum?'

She nodded and said, 'Put the radio on and listen to some music.'

'Okay.' I said and put the radio on. Some Chinese music flowed in the air. She sat up and looked very content.

'The birds still are singing. Sometimes, they wake me up.' I remembered Mother telling me that before.

'Yes, you can hear them.'

'Yes, I like to hear them sing. All these chattering.' My Mother liked the wonders of nature. In later days when our income was better, she would buy flowers to brighten the room and she would grow some nice plants.

I helped Mother to get up and have a wash. She was moving about fairly well. My Brother George and I were planning to get a wheelchair for her and I planned to buy some stronger painkiller for the pain in her leg.

I told my younger sister, Miranda, about Mother wanting to sit up and to listen to the radio. She was astonished because she did not think that our mother was well enough to do that. I was glad that my Mother recognised me. I always remember the last two times when I visited my Father before he died; he did not recognise me and thought that I was George, my brother.

My eldest sister Wah and I went to the pharmacy and bought her some stronger pain killer tablets and ointment. Later that afternoon, my brother George and I went to the Red Cross to borrow a wheelchair.

I remember that George and I went to see a movie at that time called 'Seabiscuit'. It was a true story about a horse in America that was regarded as a useless horse and someone wanted to shoot it. But fortunately, a trainer pleaded for his life and later trained the horse to be one of the most successful horses in the history of horse racing in the USA. The story also involved a rider and an owner and the trainer, all were losers to start with but with determination and will, they made it in the world. The story was sad and it made me think of Mother.

On a Thursday evening, my two younger sisters, Miranda and Sharon, were in the apartment with Mum, just talking. Mother had another stroke and her face went down in the wheelchair as if she was unconscious. We took her to bed and called the ambulance.

She was admitted to the local hospital and put on a ventilator. Because of her history and her ninety-three years, the doctors were suggesting no treatment would be given. She would be given tender loving care. We all agreed.

The following day, we went to see her in the bed and I noticed that her right leg was becoming blue; meaning that her circulation was getting worse. I was due to fly back to the UK on the Saturday and I saw Mother for the last time on the Friday. Behind the curtain were me and my Mum who was on a respirator. I gave her a kiss and said a prayer, thanking her for what she has done for me over the years. Life must have been hard with a son, living abroad for so many years.

My Mother never complained about general things and talked to us about it. In her life, she outlived two husbands and saw much sadness in the deaths of her son-in-law and daughter-in-law from cancer and a granddaughter because of a certain heart condition. She once told me that she had seen everything in her life but she was always calm. But she has also enjoyed having us, six children, with many grandchildren and great grandchildren.

She admitted that she had seen a lot of atrocities such as the Japanese occupation in Hong Kong where the Japanese killed many Chinese on the island. I do not blame her that she did not like the Japanese. We reckoned that she lived some ninety- four years because of she never a birth certificate issued. When she was younger, she always pretended to be older so that she was allowed to work and earn some money.

It was good to note that Mother did not suffer long and she died quickly without much suffering. That was a blessing.

After she died, a good friend also has lost her parents. She commented that I was an orphan, all alone in the world, like her. I replied that I never thought like that. But I realised that I was indeed all alone but thankfully I had children and wife. When I was at my lowest ebb in my career in 1995, I wished that my father was alive and he could advise me. Now, I know that all my sisters and brothers miss our mother even though she has been gone for ten years.

In a bedroom in my house, I have a picture of my Mother, looking composed and serene. In front of her, I place a flower and I know that she would like it. By the picture, there are four Chinese words of wisdom she often said. 'Whatever things come your way, meet it with peace and take it as it comes.' Ironically, I bought it at Dr. Sun's Museum (Dr. Sun is the Father of China) at Vancouver, a year after my mother's death.

*

I cannot tell of my mother without mentioning Auntie Soo. She was friend of my Mother for 89 years, since the age of five. She was a small woman and thin and was the queen at playing machong. She usually won also at machong. My Mother used to tell her off for not spending enough time to cook good foods for herself and her family of sons and daughters.

Her husband died young and she did not remarry. When telephoning in Hong Kong, there was one one-off payment and then one could ring anytime during the day or evening. So, for many years, Mother and Auntie Soo talked four times a day. She has known me and all my brothers and sisters all my life, at times praising me for visiting my parents so often. We all respected Auntie Soo and looked on her as one of the families.

Auntie Soo lived in a large apartment and she always welcomed us to play there. We always had a good time, playing and eating good food in her flat.

She and Mom were really close, and they talked endlessly on the phone. It was strange to think that many years before their deaths; they booked a gravestone near to my Dad and to each other. Auntie Soo's gravestone was not close to her husband who died many years ago. Auntie Soo was saying that all of her friends had died young and yet Soo and Mother lived the longest.

In spite of the fact that Auntie Soo never seemed to eat good food or looked after herself, she outlived Mother by one year. When I go to Hong Kong every two years or so, I always go to pay respect to our parents and ancestors. We would wipe their pictures cleanly to pay respect, including Auntie Soo's.

Tale 24

Unusual situations 1

Truth is stranger than fiction

A – Gwen's twist of fate

Gwen was a thin and old lady, aged 78 but she was active. In spite of her heart problem that she had a pacemaker in situ, she was active. She cooked for her husband and virtually did all housework and shopping for them both. She had two daughters; one lived nearby and one lived in Cornwall. But they were close and they talked frequently on the phone. Regular visits were made to keep up the close relationship.

Like many older people, they did not like changes and the house they lived in had not been altered much over the years. But they had lived well and there were good neighbours about to help or gossip with.

Then she had a mild stroke but she recovered well in the hospital. She was put on an anticoagulant drug, warfarin to thin the blood and she had to be on the medication for the rest of her life. The recovery continued and she remained fairly well and soon she was discharged home. She remained independent and made a good recovery. During the time, she had good support from the daughters and their families.

Then two years later, Gwen had a fall and fractured her hip. Doctors saw her and were not sure she was for surgery. But more importantly, Gwen did not want the operation and thought soon she would be more immobile after the surgery. She thought that she had enough of life and decided that she wanted to die. She told her family about her decisions and it was respected. The doctors were informed and they also respected her wishes. It was agreed that all her medications would be stopped, including the warfarin and digoxin. She had been on digoxin for four years by then and the tablet strengthened and lengthened her pulse.

Normally Gwen was a placid lady and did not like melodrama. Unusually she wrote to her daughters, instructing what she wanted to do with the spare bed sheets in her house and she was trying to put her things in order. Grandchildren visited her and were sad to know that the grandmother would die soon. She was frail and drank little and did not eat. The family had chosen the hymns for the funeral. The air of sadness was hanging in the air.

Three weeks went by. By a miracle, Gwen did not die but felt slightly stronger, in spite of no medication and non intervention of any kind. One day, she thought that she ought to switch off her pacemaker and finish off her life. She was undecided.

Unexpectedly, her general practitioner visited her in the hospital and they had a long conversation. No one knew of the content of the conversation but afterwards, Gwen decided to start eating again.

Doctors and the family could not believe there was such an improvement. She actually enjoyed her food and drink again. Gwen was put back on the medication. Some of her medications were changed into better or modern ones.

Gwen was eating well and soon she was tried out how to cope with life in the shelter housing unit, a part of the hospital. A few weeks went by and now, Gwen was looking better and stronger. Physiotherapy helped her and soon she was walking with a tripod.

The sheltered housing scheme was very useful to Gwen and it was planned that she would be discharged soon. The family and the medical team were baffled with the progress and they could not explain it at all.

Fate is always said to be the hunter of life but one could not hunt fate. When one wants to die, one may not be able to do so.

*

B-- Demi's tale of care

Every time I went back home to my roots in Hong Kong, I always met up with a group of old friends in a restaurant. We have known each other for more than forty years. The nine of us met and soon we talked as if we had been friends for a lifetime and we had not met only for a few weeks. We felt at ease almost instantly because we knew that we would not offend each other. We joked and talked so freely, in the best of the company.

This group of friends had been kind to me because they always wanted to pay for my share as a foreign visitor, in spite of my insistence to pay my share of the cost.

This time, I gave them all a copy of book, 'Tales from a male nurse' as a token of long friendship and thanks. Derek flicked through my book and read a page of a tale which happened to be a supernatural tale. He asked if I did believe in this supernatural story. I answered positively.

Demi said that she surely believed in this and she thought that she was different. We all looked at her intrigued. All over the years, she had never said. Then, she began to tell her tale....

Demi was a small lady and she had a very caring character. She would help people in need whenever she could. She confessed that sometimes, she could hear things from someone, not from the living and the sound floated in the air. She felt that she had an aura. She had accepted the fact that perhaps she was different.

Not long ago, she felt that she was being followed by someone. Perhaps it was a spirit. She sensed that it was a soul who was not happy. She sensed that it was a child following her and he was very lost. This went on for a week and she felt uncomfortable and she sensed that this little child needed help but she did not know what to do.

Like many Chinese, she had decided to visit the temple in Hong Kong. Wong Tai Sin was a very famous temple in Hong Kong for many years. Many Chinese went there to worship, to burn incense for the dead or the Buddha. Monks lived there in solitude and prayed to their Gods many times a day.

Demi went to speak to a monk and she told him that she was followed by a spirit, perhaps a child who was lost. The monk was kind and seemed to have come across the situation before. She has taken the advice from him to buy a paper car, a parcel which might contain some sort of direction for the spirit.

Outside her building, Demi burnt some incenses and she inserted them into the soil in a pot, along with the paper car and parcel. He bowed three times and she showed respect to the dead.

This action was not an uncommon scene in Hong Kong. Many people believed in this ceremony.

After this event, Demi no longer felt that she was being followed. The spirit of the child must have found the direction to join whoever and wherever. Demi felt a sense of peace and relief.

Demi was a helpful lady to people living in need of help and she also cared for the spirit of the dead. We all nodded in agreement that she had done a good deed.

Tale 25

Stereotyping and diversity

'The more opinion you have, the less you will see ...'
Wim Wenders

Last May, my wife and I went to Madeira for the first time. It was a beautiful place with different kinds of flowers and the climate was mild. There were flowers of different hues in the town. It was beautiful. My wife and I have never been there before and we quite liked the warmer weather. We liked to be closer to the sea too. One of the sightseeing highlights was the Monte, the highest mountain in Madeira. We had to go up by cable car.

As we were queuing, my wife noticed a rather obese woman in front of us. She was puffing and not looking very fit. She seemed to be quite an overweight lady.

We got in the same cable car along with the others. The other two ladies seemed to know this large lady and thanked her for the interesting lecture they just had on the cruise ship. This lady was some sort of lecturer on the cruise ship and she was describing the island's characteristics and special features. The other ladies were retired and enjoyed the cruising. The large lady was saying that her other special interest apart from giving lectures on the cruise ship, was diving. She was a qualified diver and has been diving for many years! It never crossed our minds that such a large and unfit looking lady could dive.

When we left the cable car, my wife confessed that she was amazed that this lady was not what she seemed and I agreed. I then quoted the word stereotyping and the concept of it was used so much in our lives. I have been teaching as a lecturer for a college for ten years and been a qualified nurse for forty years. Yet, because of the fact that I am from Hong Kong and look very Chinese, I was asked so many times in a restaurant if I was working for a Chinese restaurant nearby and even if I owned a Chinese takeaway. It felt like that I should not be a lecturer or trained nurse.

Because of the colour of my skin, once visiting a friend in Watford, I was asked by the Police if I minded being on a parade in a police station to be identified by a lady who happened to have seen a Chinese setting fire to a restaurant. I obliged and was on a parade with a few Chinese. Fortunately, the lady identified the guilty person.

Stereotyping is what we think people are and we are sometimes quite wrong in what we assume but it is easily done.

Nine years ago, I was in a cruise ship for the first time as a tourist, touring around Alaska and the British Columbia. We were enjoying the magnificent scenery and the international cuisine available from the seven restaurants. One night, my wife and I wanted to sample the best and the most expensive one for her birthday treat.

The restaurant was plush and expensively decorated and we were sitting down. We noticed that most waiters were Chinese looking and they did not seem to be too pleased to serve me. Their facial expression told the story. My wife who is English felt it too. But we ordered politely and they served us in turn with courtesy. It was a surreal experience to have felt the Chinese waiters' perception of me.

I have been working for an Awarding Body for three years as an external moderator. Before the work, we had to have a standardisation meeting at London. I always booked into the same hotel and I have been there four times over the years. They knew me and welcomed me every time I went. One summer, I thought that I could take my wife to the hotel so that we could enjoy going to theatre.

On entering the hotel, I did not know why but I told the receptionist that I was with my wife. I did not have to say this but both and my wife, who is English, and I felt that he regarded us with suspicion. He probably thought that she was my mistress and that I had a Chinese wife.

One can easily see the funny side of stereotyping. When I was learning the Yang form of taichi, the students assumed that I was the teacher because I was Chinese looking!!

Some people are very careful with people's points of view. They might think the Chinese or black people should not drive expensive cars because they are workers and could not possible afford them. Perhaps that was the reason an Asian friend of mine never went to work in his expensive car. He used to drive to work in an old banger because he did not make his colleagues envious.

Wherever a man goes, men will pursue him and paw him with their dirty institutions, and, if they can, constrain him to belong to their desperate oddfellow society.

Tale 26

A panic attack

'Everyone is more or less mad at one point.'
Rudyard Kipling

I had not seen Choi, my old friend for a long while. He was a male nurse like me. We started nursing years ago and somehow we felt a bond with each other. Very often, we went out for a Chinese meal and talked about the old times. Lately, I heard that he had been very worried about her daughter's illness.

I knocked on his door and he looked thinner than before. But he smiled and told me that things were getting better. Choi offered me some jasmine tea and we sat down and drank the fragrant liquid in his conservatory. It was good to see that he was smiling again. I enquired what had really happened. With a sign of relief, he told me his story.

Debbie, his daughter, was thirty years old. Ever since she was in high school she suffered from the odd panic attack. She was prescribed an antidepressant. Choi was not happy with it but Debbie seemed to feel better for it and tried to explain t him that the medication supplemented some form of chemical imbalance in her body. She had been on this medication for many years, though not on a high dose.

She had also been a smoker for many years also and only

gave it up after the birth of her daughter some three years ago. Unfortunately, she suffered from severe post natal depression for many months, so she started smoking again. Things were starting to look better for Debbie; she felt more in control of her life.

Then she thought that she ought to reduce her medication. She consulted the doctor and it was agreed that it was a good idea. For several weeks, she coped well with the reduced antidepressant. Now, Debbie also thought of reducing her smoking.

She went to the smoke cessation clinic for advice. The smoking cessation clinic did not appreciate the long history of her medication though they thought that it was a good idea to reduce her smoking.

For three days, Debbie was feeling okay. She was pleased with the progress.

On a Wednesday morning Debbie talked happily and told Choi and his wife that she had not smoked for two days and was coping well. Her parents were happy with Debbie's voluntary action of trying to curb her smoking as well as her reducing the medication.

On the same evening, Debbie rang Choi's wife ten times on the mobile phone pleading that she was feeling panicky and ill. She said that she could not cope with looking after her daughter. She was feeling listless and could not even get out of bed. She felt that an air of lifelessness had overwhelmed her. Straight away her mother went to stay with her and found her looking poorly and was very distressed.

Fortunately Debbie's daughter was fine and loved being looked after by her grandmother. Choi was very upset on the phone talking to Debbie because she sounded so tearful and sad. Debbie was pleading to Choi not to visit her till she was better. Debbie said that she did not want Choi to see her like so.

Her husband was working all the time and was not often at home. Choi found himself so helpless and worried. Debbie normally was the liveliest of his four children. No one seemed to know what was happening. Why had Debbie suddenly become so panicky and sombre?

The local emergency team of psychiatric nurses were very helpful. Debbie's own nurse was understanding and easy to talk to. According to the Community Psychiatric Nurse, it seemed that one should not reduce medication and stop smoking at the same time. It caused some chemical imbalances in the body that made Debbie so listless.

The episode of illness was frightening. Never had Choi seen his daughter so quiet and sad and lifeless. Debbie herself felt it too and she cried so sadly and easily. She did not sleep well and had no interest in food. In addition, she did not want to do anything, not even driving for thirty minutes. At times, Choi's wife had to bully Debbie to get out of bed and get dressed.

It was fortunate that Choi's wife was retired and was there looking after their granddaughter so Debbie's husband could work and to make a living.

Eventually Debbie was put on more medication and went to counselling and was under the care of mental nurses and psychiatrist. She started smoking again. It took two months to see her with a very slight improvement. Choi, his wife and Debbie's husband were all very worried.

Choi said to me that at times, he feared that Debbie would not get better at all and he felt so sad and helpless. Four months on, Choi and his wife drove Debbie and granddaughter to a cottage by the sea, to enjoy some quiet time and the bracing sea air. However, Debbie's health did not improve. This made Choi and his wife very worried. When Choi gave Debbie a hug to bid goodbye, he was wondering if she would get better. Debbie was just not herself, so subdued and quiet, not her normal self at all.

The company she worked for was very understanding whilst she was off sick. Her boss seemed to have suffered similar illness before and understood her situation. Moreover, Debbie had many good friends to support her via emails and facebook. Natalie has been growing up with Debbie since they were little girls and she was most supportive. She visited her often at home and talked to her with love and care and encouragement.

Fortunately, three weeks later, Choi drove to visit Debbie and he found her a different person, chatty and seemingly much happier. Debbie came out of the house to give him a hug which had not happened for so long. Debbie was on the road to recovery. Choi could not believe he was witnessing such an improvement, after four long months.

Debbie knew that she had been very ill. She was very thankful for the help from her parents, especially her mother.

Choi wiped a tear as he was telling me this true tale of the unexpected and very sudden illness. We had learnt that one must not reduce medication at the same time as stopping smoking. Choi was grateful that Debbie was feeling better and was now on the way to full recovery.

It is said that depression, anxiety and panic attacks are signs of weaknesses. In fact, they are signs of trying to be strong for too long. One in three of us go through this episode in life. It is quite normal to have a nervous breakdown

Tale 27

My Father

'Memories are like stones, time and distance erode them with acid'
Bettie Ugo

My father was born in Hong Kong in November, 1920. I was told that his elder brother and his father were also born in Hong Kong. I never met my grandfather but he had two wives and my father and his elder brother were both born to the first wife of my grandfather. My grandfather was an office assistant in the Urban Service Department when he retired. And father took over his position after his retirement.

My father's elder brother was 'a dresser', a care assistant. He joined the National China regime under Cheung Kai Sheik in the care division in the 1940s. When Cheung was defeated, he stayed in China and served for Chairman Mao as a foot doctor, a kind of nurse-doctor for many years. Later, he had gained the status as a Chinese doctor in the Communist China for many years. When he retired, he was treated well by the State having a good pension and free housing. I always wonder if that was the reason father and mother made no objection to my going into nursing, though they never told me about my uncle's past nursing history.

My father was a progressive man in that he went to night

school to learn to speak and write English. He had a very good and clear handwriting, better than mine. He always taught us to learn and study English because he thought that it was the language of the future. He took us to see many English movies, like 'The bridge of River Kwai' directed by the illustrious English director, David Lean, to learn good English. Perhaps that was the reason that I have always been a movie fan. I saw many movies in my younger days at 17.30, a time slot that was the cheapest and my brother and I saw many a good film and perhaps that was the reason that our English was comparatively good. We saw many classic movies made by David Lean and some John Wayne films.

My father used to play with my mother when they were little. When my father knew that my mother to go to a blind date, in order to be married off to another Chinese so that my mother would not be a financial burden to her family, my father was very upset and he walked from Hong Kong to Canton (Kwanchow) in 2 days and two nights. He had to sleep rough for two nights to find his elder brother.

My uncle (my father's elder brother) looked after my father for many days till he recovered from his upset and took him back to Hong Kong to work. My Mother's first marriage produced three children but her first husband and eldest son died suddenly from cholera.

My father wanted to marry my mother but he had strong opposition from his family because my mother was a married woman with children and was nine years older than him. But he was a stubborn man and must have loved my mother very much. They married and started life together. They had four children and I was the youngest son with one elder brother and two younger sisters. However, my father was very good to mother's other two children, Cheuck and Wah. He always treated them like my own brother and sister.

My father borrowed money to fund brother Cheuck to learn driving. Cheuck was thankful and knew my father was very good to him and he changed his surname to Poon. Many years later, my father had a stroke and was bedridden for many years. Cheuck would go daily to carry him from bed to the wheelchair and back as a token of thanks for what my father had done for him.

However, my father was a hot tempered man. Despite of the fact that he was a small and thin man, he would slap us across the face if we misbehaved. His grandchildren and we were all afraid of him. We never got too close to him. When we were older, we wanted to talk to him but he was a drinking man then and one could not reason with him when he was under the influence of alcohol. In fact, he was an embarrassment when he was drunk, being hot tempered and talking loudly in public. Poor mother had much to put up with. Perhaps that was the reason my brothers and sisters and I do not drink very much at all and we dislike people drinking heavily.

But my father was a righteous man and not corruptible. He worked in the Urban Services Department for most of his life and most of the staff was bribed by shopkeepers so that they could extend their business. But my father would not take money from them and he was mocked by his colleagues. Perhaps that was the reason we were quite poor.

Seven of us used to live in one room and my elder brother even had to sleep in the corridor for many years. However, we were relatively less poor when one compared with others nearby because my father was a foreman. We relished playing football, table tennis and playing on a spacious community ground.

Father would encourage us to eat more and be strong. In the hot summers, occasionally he would take mother and us and hired a sampan to go out to the sea to enjoy our cold bottles of coca cola and cup cakes. I often think of his small frame and thin face, relishing the cool breeze from the sea.

One stroke of fortune came to father in early 1960s. He was asked if he wanted to take a piece of paper out of a straw hat to see if he was entitled to a flat. He was lucky and we moved from Wanchai, Hong Kong to Shamshuipo, Kowloon, ten minutes walk to the ferry and the sea. Our flat had three bedrooms, a kitchen and a big lounge and for the first time, we could afford a television.

My father was a right wing person, disliking Chairman's Mao's cruelty. We often saw corpses floating on the sea around Hong Kong. They were the unfortunates who tried to escape from China so that they could find food to eat and a place to live. In the 1960s, I remember well that for a few months, there were conflicts between the right wing and the left wing Chinese in Hong Kong. One famous radio broadcaster who was outspoken was bombed and killed in his car by some extremist Chinese. The curfews frightened me. At nights, we were not allowed to go out because there were battles between the Chinese. Fortunately, we lived not by the main road but I could hear the noise of conflict from the main roads.

It was said that because of my father could not be bribed, he was framed and this contributed to his request for early retirement. He knew that in the building where we lived, we were the poorest because of his refusal to bribery. I could not remember if he had any close friends.

When I was little, I could not tell if father favoured boys over girls. I recall some tender moments when he would take me by the hand when I was little and bought me a nice pear. It was peeled nicely by the shopkeeper and father asked if it was sweet.

He was a very progressive because he and mother had no objection when I wanted to marry an English girl.

I could not recall that he had many friends. Perhaps he was too righteous and did not mix with people who liked to take bribes. When he retired at the age of fifty, he did manage to take a holiday abroad in Taiwan, this he did enjoy and had a good time. Sadly that was his last holiday abroad because soon after he had a stroke.

It was strange to think that before the episode of stroke, father was never ill. He smoked for the most of life and he drank heavily from morning to night for some years. He had very chauvinistic and no one dared question him. I remember that he liked to drink and eat in the local restaurant, listening to some Chinese singers.

In 1977, whilst he was walking uphill to a voting session that he had a stroke. He did not die but remained bedridden for eleven years. I remember it well in 1997 when I heard the bad news at Kettering. I felt helpless and useless. In those days, there were no mobile phones and one could not ring us easily as like nowadays. The sudden bad news affected all of us. Living so faraway made me feel so helpless. I remember that at times, I would wake up suddenly in a pool of sweat, thinking of what I could do to help.

He could speak a little but he was half paralysed. My mother, brothers and sisters became his carers. Two years on, they asked me if they should allow him smoke again. I said they should because he had no enjoyment in life. Smoking certainly did give him some relief. I visited him every two years.

I went home to attend his funeral and it was strange that I carried his ashes in an urn in my hands. Such is the fragility of life. My father's life and his parents' were a mystery to us. There were many things that we did not know. We could not recall much talk from him about his parents. I would dearly like to know what he liked to eat best, his favourite singer and movie. Was his family rich and what was his father like? What really happened that caused him to retire so early? Being a grandfather myself, I would like to know what my grandfather was like.

During the research into my parents' life, I came to realise that the Poon's province was a rich and pleasant province in Canton (Kwanchow). As I had never been there, I went to visit the Poon's province with my sister in October, 2013. It was a prosperous place, with Poon's public transport and restaurants and a lovely lake nearby. My sister showed me the location where my father's elder brother lived (the one who was a foot doctor). A sudden feeling came to me and I wished that I had met him, someone from the caring side of my family. I would have liked to ask him about the nursing and the medical care of those bygone days and perhaps have a drink together.

Tale 28

Unusual situations 2

'Once the people start to reason, all is lost.'

A Jon, the consultant in orthodontics

Jon had been working in the same hospital for thirty five years. He loved his job as a specialist consultant in orthodontics. After many years working in the same hospital, he became the leader of the unit and he was very good in what he did. The staff liked him.

He only did his private practice on Saturdays. He had a lovely large house in town and another one in the country, three expensive cars and a boat. He had always been an efficient worker and could deal with more patients than his younger consultants who seemed to do their quota of work and then head for the golf course or deal with their private patients.

On his sixty-third birthday, he felt unwell with a feeling of general malaise. He had a check up and nothing abnormal was detected but felt that he should slow down. He thought he would retire and would go back to work part time perhaps, two days a week to keep his hand in. His retirement request was accepted and he received a lump sum of almost a million pounds and with a good monthly income.

Amongst his relatives and family he was the one earning the most. He took them on holidays and paid for everyone.

After a time he was not feeling too well so he went to see a doctor friend of his. He was examined more closely and was recommended to have more tests. The tests confirmed his worst fear, as it showed that he was suffering from cancer of the prostate gland with secondary growths.

Jon's world was shattered. He was informed that it was not operable and that he might have a year or two to live. He was depressed and crying at home when he was not working. He was not in great pain but he was feeling very low. When he took his boat out to the sea, he found that he could not appreciate the quietness of nature. He was not happy and he could not enjoy his holidays abroad.

His wife was also retired and with a very agreeable pension and lump sum of money. Like Jon, she was not used to not working and so she became a volunteer in the same hospital. The material things of cars, boat and expensive holiday did not make them happy.

Jon found himself happiest at work despite his illness. He was very good at what he did. His patients loved him for the care and kindness he showed and the nurses liked him and enjoyed working with him. The sense of satisfaction and respect from others meant very much to him.

Jon started working for three more extra days of the week, saying he was there to catch up with his paperwork. He offered to help other doctors and he looked after those patients for them very well. The doctors felt that he needed things to do, what he could do best and they made him happy, even though he was not paid for these three days of the week. Jon did not care about the money as he was already quite well off.

The senior managers of the hospital were aware of this practice and they realised Jon was seeing more patients than his colleagues, thus making more income for the Trust. The hospital knew they did not have to pay him and it was a win-win situation for everyone.

His wife was observing this practice and she could not believe his happiness at work and yet when Jon went home in the evenings after work, he would start crying over his misfortune. He was inconsolable.

He regretted that he did not have long to live and would not have more time to be with his children. His material possession meant nothing to him. He slept irregularly. He was afraid that he would be in constant pain soon and he did not want a lingering death. Now, all he wanted was to work on.

This went on for a year. One Wednesday, Jon had a heart attack at work and he collapsed on the floor in his office and he knew that he was going to die .But his facial expression conveyed a thousand words: he felt that he was lucky to have such a good job, helping so many patients get better and it has given him satisfaction and respect. Moreover, he got what he wished for, to die almost instantly at work.

B. TNP house

In the year 2000, I was an outreach tutor for the NVQ training. I went to many care homes to teach and assess students to pass the National Vocational qualification in the Health and Social Care. I must have been to some one hundred care homes and taught many students. I enjoyed the challenge enormously. Most of the students were carers with low pay and most had not many academic qualifications.

Many homes were private enterprises and most owners were in for the profit and were quite mean. The students seemed to like to tell me all the gossips of the homes: some of them had even no official contracts of employment. Some advised me to use the milk on the right hand side of the refrigerator in the kitchen because the milk on the other side was all diluted with water to save money and they were for the residents. At some homes, even potatoes were rationed for the residents. No wonder that there were great turnover in some homes and one could see many staff come and go.

But the TNP house was very different. It was owned by a very good hearted lady called Jay. She had studied and passed the NVQ level 3 and 4 and she was a very caring person. The carers were my students and they had studied level 2, and then 3 and then 4 with my help. I was teaching and assessing in the home for five years and trained nearly all the staff.

The residents seemed comfortable and felt well cared for. The relatives were happy and appreciated the help from the staff and the owner who was also the manager. Jay told me that she would provide whatever needed for the best care for the residents though the profit from the home was not great.

Her kindness to the staff was appreciated that they knew that they were fortunate to work there providing good quality services to the residents even though they were on the minimum wage. At my training session in their lounge, Jay always brought us tea and biscuits and she supported the training whole heartedly. She knew that if the staff were better trained, they could provide good care. Her staff would appreciate the reasons for the policies and the procedures of the home. It was the happiest home that I had been to teach and assess and it was a pleasure to see the human kindness and care for the vulnerable.

It was good to see the Social Services were aware of the good care the home had provided and the home had a good reputation. It was a shame that seeing care homes providing good care with the owners' support was such a rarity.

C. Lee's malaena-1988

Rena and Jack always enjoyed holidaying in Cornwall. They loved bodysurfing on the sea and spent a lot of time on the beach. They would hire a cottage every year and spent most of the time relaxing. They relished the sea air and the scenic surrounding of the rugged Cornwall, especially away from their nursing work and the busy city life. Rena was a part time midwife and Jack was a nursing officer in surgery at a general hospital.

Lee was their son, one year old and full of energy. He enjoyed the frolics by the sea, building sandcastle with the parents. He loved jumping over the waves with them.

The two weeks of holiday soon finished. They were now heading back home to the midlands.

On the first day, Lee was feeling not quite right. He normally slept well but on the night, he was restless and made little murmurs of cry. Rena thought he might be wet, so she changed his nappy. She saw his stool was blood stained and it frightened her. During the following day, Lee ate his food okay and drank fine. But he had another blood stained motion. He began to look pale.

Jack and Rena were worried and took Lee to see the general practitioner. Instantly, Lee was sent to the paediatric ward of the local hospital for admission. His haemoglobin was low which was not surprising as he had two bleeds. He was instantly put on blood transfusion to supplement his blood loss. But all the other tests and X-ray were normal. The consultant saw Lee and was unsure of the diagnosis. The parents told the doctors that Lee had been eating well and nothing unusual happened during the holiday.

A surgeon was asked to examine Lee and found his abdomen was not tender nor there were any signs of growth and pain.

Jack was working in the same hospital as a nursing officer. He was worried that no diagnosis was made. It appeared that everything was normal except the low red blood cells count. Lee had two bleeds but since then his bowel movement had been normal. Did he eat something from the beach that cut his gut and cause the bleeding? The doctors were not sure.

Because Jack was quite senior in the hospital and the patient was so young, the medical team discussed the action at length. The surgeon was keen on doing a laporatomy to explore what was wrong but the medical director was not keen.

One day had gone and Lee had received two units of blood and was feeling better. His haemoglobin was now normal and he seemed fine. The medical team had decided to transfer him to Birmingham Children hospital for more tests and observation.

At the Children's hospital, Lee was admitted and the history revealed that his family did not have any history of rectal bleeding and he was looking fine. All the tests revealed nothing abnormal was detected. Jack and Rena were worried. Should they suggest any operation to see what was wrong inside? Further x-rays and scans were normal. The parents stayed overnight in the hospital in turn to be with Lee.

Lee was examined and seen by two more specialist consultants. Again, nothing conclusive was diagnosed and no treatment was prescribed, except further observation.

Lee was behaving normally, eating and drinking okay with no signs of further bleeding. When his parents looked around on the ward, they realised how ill the other children were. Lee often went down to the hospital playground to play because he was bored.

Lee had become a mystery to the medical team. After a long weekend on observation, Lee' daily living was normal and he was discharged.

For the next twenty six years, Lee was growing up with no further bleeding. His episode of bleeding remained a mystery to his parents. Jack, the father, liked cogitating, one of his favourite past times but he could not think of the reason for his son's bleeding. He assumed that he had to accept life was mysterious and something just could not be resolved.

Tale 29

A small research into male nurses, general nursing in the NHS

'Basic research is like shooting an arrow into the air and, when it lands, painting a target'
Homer Adkins

In the world of nursing in England, there are many allocations of trainee nurses and trained nurses on the wards and departments. They are not permanent staff. They come and go. It is not easy to keep up with friendship on a long term basis. I have a handful of friends who are trained general nurses and thankfully we do keep in touch.

With the publication of my first book, I went to facebook to publicize it. As a result, I did gain contact with more male nurses. Most of us are retired or semi-retired. A few weeks ago, an idea came to me to conduct a small research into the male nurses in general nursing. As I mentioned in my first book, most male nurses work in psychiatry but there are not many male nurses in general nursing, especially those who have been working all our working lives in that sphere.

My questions are personal but direct. It might be probing and I can appreciate if the friends do not wish to answer.

The questions are:

1 When is the happiest time in your career in nursing and why?

2 When is the worst time in nursing and the reasons?

3 Would you start nurse training again if you were living your life again?

4 Any other comments.

All men asked to join the research have been in nursing for more than forty years and most are retired. Ten men are asked and three did not give me any feedback. I appreciate that they are personal questions; especially I knew some male nurses were unfortunate in their career that some were made redundant or some had a not smooth career because of reorganisations. Some did not want to talk about it at all.

One or two answered my research by emails. I sensed from the others that they might find it difficult to write it down. Hence, I rang them up and we had more meaningful discussions with my old friends. They did feel chatty and liked talking about their past lives.

These were the findings:

Happiest times in the nursing career:

These male nurses had a diverse background. One started in the Air Force as a general nurse. One did the general nursing training but in due course, he was in a voluntary job of helping others in need at St. Johns Ambulance for more than forty years. Two were general nurses and trained mental nurses but later on in the career, they went into personnel department (nowadays, it is called the human resource department).

Three men felt that the best times were when they were newly qualified, doing the clinical work. We had relatively less responsibilities and could pass on queries to senior staff. One felt good about his clinical expertise and later specialised in intensive care. He felt much rewarded by patients recovering well from intensive care. He felt so blessed and rewarded by what he did in the St. Johns' Ambulance. One male nurse felt happy when he was in the Air Force because he had great responsibilities and liked it. In those days, he was taught and performed electrocardiogrammes and did blood test procedures. It was good to note that four men out of seven who answered the research felt that the good times outweighed the bad times.

Yet the remaining men felt unsure what the best times were. It was interesting to note that one male nurse started in mental nursing first because the main reason was that he had accommodation provided for and pay, otherwise he might have been on the streets. He had a great time in mental nursing and continued in general nursing. Later on, he diversified into personnel management.

It might be interesting to note the backgrounds of these male nurses before they retired were in education, human resources, health authorities, senior management and clinical general nursing.

The worst times in nursing:

However, the worst times were quite horrendous. One was involved with a colleague who was linked to malpractice and a murder in clinical nursing. The price to pay was heavy, with stress and sleepless nights and turmoil of involving the police and court cases. He survived the ordeal but learnt later that they really ought to have supported each others as nurses.

Reorganisations were the phases of life in the NHS and it certainly affected many members of staff, including male nurses. One became ill and he was recovering in a mental clinic and others paid the price of losing the jobs with a deep resentment of the NHS. One was senior and fortunate enough to have stayed and was treated successfully in a mental clinic himself, courtesy from the NHS. He was amazed at meeting so many stressed-out employees from the NHS at the centre. Luckily, he survived it and thrived on his experiences to teach at a college.

One male nurse was involved in a disciplinary procedure that lasted four years. In the fourth year, he thought that he would be demoted and was in fear of what he could do in the future. But all these procedures led to no avail. But he lived through the stress for so long with no support other than his family. It was the worst time in his career. For one male nurse in the Air Force, the worst time was when a young patient died from conflict. What a waste of a young life as a casualty of war, he thought. The impact of the bad times in nursing amongst the male nurses was huge. One male nurse did feel the constant organisations made staff behave like dog eating dogs, making people behave in the worst ways.

Highlights of the nursing career:

One man had met the Pope and the Queen; one met Prince Charles and Prince Edward and one man was taught by a tutor who was the student of Evelyn Pearce, a well known writer who wrote nursing text books in the old days.

One male nurse felt constant reward when he helped to airlift patients or victims from dangerous situations when working for the St. John Ambulance. He later became a commander in that service.

Would these male nurses be advocates to encourage men into nurse training?

Three men would go in nurse training again because it is still a rewarding job. Some were not so sure because the conditions are so much worse and some would certainly not recommend nursing again.

In summary, it is lamentable to note that only few men (about 35%) have enjoyed their lives in nursing with more seeming to have a bad time in the NHS. Although this is a small scale research into male nursing, yet it reveals some information on us, male nurses, a feeling of negativity. This reminds me of once, not so long time, I was happy teaching in the college for health and social care and when I said that I would be an advocate for nursing, I was instantly reprimanded that I should not have done because there were so many newly-trained nurses unable to find a job and generally, nursing was in a bad state. But deep inside, I feel that with more people living longer, there is a desperate need to have nurses trained to look after them.

Tale 30

My view of the NHS in the last forty years

'The power of accurate observation is commonly called cynicism by those who have not got it.'

As this is the last chapter of my tales, I think that I ought to look back over the last forty years that I have been in England, to assess the progress and changes. This is not a comprehensive look at all issues only my own birds-eye view on some topics I am interested in. Some may be my cynical view on things.

1 Legal issues …I was amazed when reading the newspaper, 'The Independent' to learn that out of the NHS budget which amounted to billions of pounds, one fifth was spent on compensation to patients for medical errors in maternal units. This amounted to millions of pounds and it is sad to think of this waste of money.

2 Bed closure …in my years in the NHS, many beds have been closed and hospitals have been shut and sold off, especially the large mental hospitals so that the patients could be looked after in the community. Where has all that gone? Cottage or convalescent hospitals had also been closed also, and this led to shortage of beds.

3 Parking …It is sad to think that years ago car parking was easy and free. Now it is expensive to park our cars in the hospitals and sometimes, there is no space for parking.

Hospitals earn a lot of money by charging for parking but one might wonder if it is right or wrong to do this.

In 2013, a study by the Health and Social care Information Centre found some NHS organisations were charging three times the national average parking fee.

4 Specialisation and grading of staff …In the 1960s and 1970s we had many generalists who knew about many aspects of medical and nursing knowledge. Since then there are so many specialisms such as diabetic specialists, moving and handlers, palliative nurses, computer nurses and gastroscopy specialist nurses. It seems that with so many types of specialists, the generalists have become second class citizens.

However because of specialisation, things have improved. It is remarkable to see the improvement in eye surgery such as the treatment of cataracts and glaucoma. When I first nursed eye patients following surgery some thirty years ago, patients had to wear dark glasses post operatively and the nursing we did is now obsolete. In heart surgery, there seemed to be significant improvement also. Cardiac catheterisation and insertion of stents were uncommon thirty years ago.

Because of this job specialisation payment of the staff became more expensive as salaries increased and grading became an issue. Some clinical jobs became downgraded. Some jobs were done by care assistants- jobs that used to be done by nurses. Care assistants were paid less than trained nurses. Doctors used to perform gastroscopies but this procedure was now done by a nurse specialist. Such nurses were paid less than doctors.

5 Risk assessments … The rise in compensation payments costing NHS dear explains the rise of risk assessment. Such is the increase in the workload that risk assessment has become a

bugbear. These are risk assessments for health and safety issues such as lifting of patients, fire procedure and the prevention of pressure sores. It seems that nowadays, no one is allowed to do anything before it is properly risk assessed.

6 The rise for business managers …From the 1990's, with the development of the NHS Community Care Act., all hospitals were becoming trusts. Medical consultants and senior nurses had to work with business managers. The NHS developed a so-called internal market, purchasing and selling services. Has it been a success? Newspapers report that many trusts or foundation hospitals are in the red.

Paul was the head of a surgical prosthesis department and his boss was a business manager and she cared only for the profit of the department and was unaware of the quality of the service delivered. Paul and his staff worked very hard by doing extra work privately to earn income for the department. Paul and other staff got no rewards for the extra work and his department was not even rewarded with a new piece of equipment. Pressures were put on Paul to do extra work to earn more private income. He was not happy and he contacted the legal department of the hospital to see if he would be properly insured to do this private work. The solicitor was not sure. But the business manager took no notice and she wanted Paul to do the extra work.

7 Decrease of pay …Performance related pay has been around for many years. Staff are given a set of priorities to achieve their target. If a member of staff does well, he might be rewarded with a bonus. But many staff members are at the maximum of their pay scale and if they do not achieve the performance target, they will not get any extra pay or the bonus. But in the past two years, things have become worse.

If a member of staff does not achieve the targets he or she will be downgraded. This will also affect the pension. Coercion from the bosses is fierce. The unions are not happy. Would the bosses just downgrade most staff so that the government does not have to hand out more pension to them?

From the ex-colleagues I meet over the last years, I gather there is a sense of fear or paranoia at work. Staff seems feeling insecure as if some one is looking over their shoulder all the time. Certainly, the sense of loyalty is not like it used to be.

In one of the tales I wrote about a small research project I carried out with. In summary it transpires that most did not want to work for the NHS any more. Poor publicity appears in newspaper almost daily. Why has the NHS gone so wrong? Many years on, the NHS remains a political football, changing almost constantly. There is no opportunity to allow time to settle the change.

It may be easy for me to say. The constant changes in the NHS cannot be good for the NHS. It takes time for changes to make effect. Why can the political parties get together to agree on a long term strategy, like ten or fifteen years' plan, to allow a policy to settle and to take effects?

30A

The sea and I

I must see the sea again as I have not seen it for a while,
to watch the boats heading home, and the stars to guide them by.
I miss its surging tide and the seagulls flying by,
the beautiful hues of the setting sun, casting on the children
paddling their feet having so much fun.
How lovely is the sound of the rolling waves towards the sands!
The beauty of nature never ends.
I could easily fall asleep on the sands,
feeling composed as if the world will always stand.
We have been friends for a long while, the sea and I,
living through life's ups and downs, leading a vagrant gipsy life.

November, 2013- France
Patrick K S Poon